DANGER, DOLPHINS, AND GINGER BEER

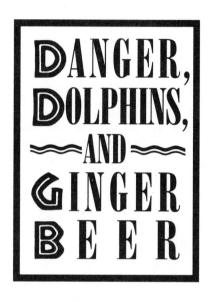

DANGER, DOLPHINS, AND GINGER BEER

By John Vigor

Atheneum   1993   New York

Maxwell Macmillan Canada
Toronto

Maxwell Macmillan International
New York   Oxford   Singapore   Sydney

Atheneum
Macmillan Publishing Company
866 Third Avenue
New York, NY 10022

Maxwell Macmillan Canada, Inc.
1200 Eglinton Avenue East
Suite 200
Don Mills, Ontario M3C 3N1

Macmillan Publishing Company is part of the Maxwell Macmillan Communication Group of Companies.

First edition

Printed in the United States of America

10 9 8 7 6 5 4 3 2 1
Library of Congress Cataloging-in-Publication Data
Vigor, John.
    Danger, dolphins, and ginger beer / John Vigor.—1st ed.
        p.   cm.
    Summary: While camping on Crab Island in the British Virgin Islands, twelve-year-old Sally and her two younger brothers rescue an injured dolphin and become involved in a dangerous adventure with mysterious strangers.
    ISBN 0–689–31817–0
    [1. Dolphins—Fiction. 2. Boats and boating—Fiction. 3. British Virgin Islands—Fiction. 4. Brothers and sisters—Fiction. 5. Mystery and detective stories.] I. Title.
PZ7.V6725Do   1993
[Fic]—dc20   92–26182

To June

CONTENTS

1	The Dying Dolphin	1
2	Fighting Talk	13
3	Problems at the Hospital	27
4	*Redwing* Runs into Trouble	41
5	Daniel's Surprise	52
6	*White Lightning's* Disaster	66
7	A Foster Mother for DJ	76
8	Andy Goes Solo	88
9	Mysterious Visitors	98
10	Gloria Pays a Visit	107
11	Kidnapped!	117
12	Shipwreck!	128
13	Preparing to Escape	139
14	*Freebooter* under Fire	149
15	The Secret of the Fender	161
16	Family Reunions	170

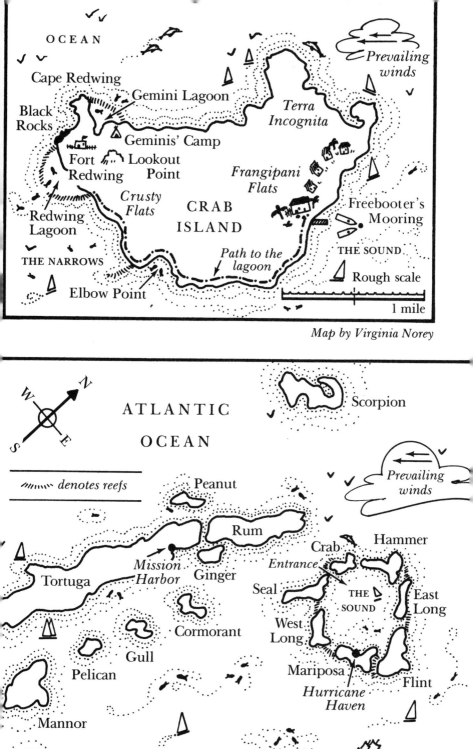

OCEAN

Cape Redwing

Gemini Lagoon

Black
Rocks

Geminis' Camp

*Terra
Incognita*

Fort
Redwing

Lookout
Point

*Frangipani
Flats*

*Crusty
Flats*

CRAB
ISLAND

Redwing
Lagoon

Freebooter's
Mooring

THE SOUND

THE NARROWS

*Path to the
lagoon*

Rough scale

Elbow Point

1 mile

*Prevailing
winds*

Map by Virginia Norey

ATLANTIC

OCEAN

Scorpion

*Prevailing
winds*

denotes reefs

Peanut

Rum

Hammer

Crab

Mission
Harbor

Entrance

Ginger

Seal

THE
SOUND

East
Long

Tortuga

West
Long

Cormorant

Pelican

Gull

Mariposa

Flint

*Hurricane
Haven*

Mannor

1

THE DYING DOLPHIN

Sally Grant grinned happily as a wave smacked against *Redwing*'s bows and splashed white spray on her cheeks. She was enjoying the voyage back to Crab Island.

They were under full sail, she and her loyal crew, Peter. This was how ships had carried cargo in the old days, when these islands were full of pirates and buccaneers.

Redwing's cargo today was fruit and vegetables, eggs and flashlight batteries, fresh from the bustling port of Mission Harbor just across the channel. It was a cargo badly needed by the defenders of Fort Redwing.

Sally ducked her head and missed another dollop of spray. She sailed small boats as naturally as other kids rode bikes. The Grant family had always loved sailing. And out here in the calm tropical waters of the British Virgin Islands, the Caribbean sea was warm and blue and friendly.

She licked her lips, and her tongue tingled with the taste of warm salt. The trade wind was blowing against *Redwing*, sending armies of puffy white clouds to march overhead. But the little open sailboat was making good progress, tacking in long zigzags toward Crab Island, where they were camping.

Now and then a harder puff of wind made the boat heel over and Sally tugged at the tiller to keep it going straight.

She did it automatically. But this time, as she pulled the tiller to windward, it made her think.

Sailing a boat was a lot like looking after your brothers. You had to keep tugging at them all the time to keep them going straight, too.

Somehow you could never trust them to do the right thing on their own. And—just like the boat— the moment you stopped tugging, everything started getting out of control.

A frown flitted across her face. Ever since her mom died eighteen months earlier, just after Sally's eleventh birthday, Sally had been trying to take her place. But it hadn't been easy.

When you tugged at a boat to keep it going

straight, it didn't mind. When you tugged at your brothers—well, anything could happen.

Now, as the wind fell light again, Sally looked at the growing shape of the island ahead and decided it was time to make another tack. *Redwing*'s tall, red-brown sails shivered as the fourteen-foot dinghy went through the eye of the wind, paused, heeled over on the other side, and gathered speed again.

Sally watched her brother Peter pull in the smaller front sail, the jib, and move across the boat to sit down on the other side. Then she, too, sat down next to him, enjoying the feel of the sun-warmed wooden seat against her bare legs.

"How far to Crab Island, Mr. Mate?" she asked.

Peter shaded his eyes with a hand and squinted into the sun. "About two miles, I guess. You can see Lookout Point now."

Lookout Point was the highest spot on the tiny island. On their first day at Fort Redwing, after they had set up their tent in a clearing in the bush near Black Rocks, they had all walked up to the top of a steep hill nearby.

They named it Lookout Point. And, like explorers seeing an undiscovered ocean for the first time, they had given names to all the islands laid out before them.

Lookout Point was where her youngest brother, eight-year-old Andy, was supposed to be keeping watch right now. She wondered if he'd spotted the catamaran.

"I hope Andy's all right," she said.

Peter shrugged. "Sure. He'll be okay."

"Yes, but I mean I hope it was all right to leave him there alone."

"Someone had to keep watch."

"Yes, but what if the catamaran came back?"

Peter linked his fingers and stretched his arms slowly. "He'd just stay right where he was if he had any sense," he said. "He wouldn't try to fight them on his own."

Sally hoped Peter was right. You never knew with Andy, though. He was impulsive, sometimes. Dad always said she and Andy came out of the same mold.

Peter was dreamy and good-natured. He was ten years old but almost as tall as she was. He was wide-eyed and had dark brown hair like Dad's. He was really intelligent. But when you said something he didn't like, he'd get uncomfortably quiet.

Andy, on the other hand, had fair hair just like hers. They'd both inherited their mother's blue eyes. And Andy was just plain bouncy. If he didn't like something, he niggled and twitched and fought until he wore you down and you gave in.

Before she had left that morning she had warned him just to watch for the twins and not to get involved if they raided the camp. And he had set out solemnly for Lookout Point with a school notebook for his official log and a backpack containing two sandwiches and a bottle of ginger beer.

But he didn't always listen to her. She could imagine him up there on top of Lookout Point, where he could see all over Crab Island and far out over the warm, blue sea.

Right now he'd be snuggled down in the long, dry, sweet-smelling grass under the wispy casuarina tree. It was the perfect place for a lookout. And Andy had definite ideas about how to be a lookout.

Only his head would stick above the grass. And if he kept his head perfectly still, it would look like a rock against the skyline. He'd read that in some book or other.

Sally peered up at Lookout Point in the distance. She could see the casuarina tree swaying gently in the northeast trade wind, but there was nothing beneath it that looked like a rock.

She wondered if he'd saved some ginger beer for later, or whether he'd drunk it all in one go as usual. "Drink half now and save the rest for later." If she'd told him once, she'd told him fifty times.

Dad had taught them to make ginger beer when they lived in England. It wasn't really beer, of course. It was like root beer, only made with ginger. It was good and fizzy and the bubbles tickled your nose when you drank it.

Andy said the best part was when the hot taste of ginger made your throat catch on fire. She could picture him up there drinking his bottle of ginger beer, the whole thing in one go, lying sideways so the bottle wouldn't show above the grass and give him away.

Not that he needed to be so careful. The island was only three miles long and two miles wide, and it was pretty much deserted.

A small resort hotel with twelve beach bungalows clung low to the ground on the eastern coast, where the cooling trade wind came whistling across the sound to rattle the coconut palms fringing the white beach.

And that was all, apart from two campsites on the opposite coast. The better of the two was where they'd raised their tent. They had christened it Fort Redwing, after their sailboat.

It was a level site on grass just above the beach and it had its own small lagoon protected by a coral reef. There was a narrow gap in the reef where they could get *Redwing* in and out any time they liked.

The other campsite, about half a mile away on the western side of the island, was smaller and rougher and there was no break in the coral. That meant you could only get a boat in or out at high tide, when the reef was covered with water. And the tide was only high enough for an hour or two a day.

Sally smiled as she remembered Dad asking her which campsite they'd prefer to use while he was away, attending his medical conference in New York. She hadn't had to think twice. They had packed their tent and camping things into the dinghy and sailed straight to Fort Redwing.

And everything had been wonderful until the day before yesterday.

It had happened in the afternoon, while Sally was helping Andy practice putting his head under water in the lagoon. He was learning how to swim.

Another sailboat came barging into their lagoon.

It was a Hobie 14 catamaran and it came in fast, skimming through the narrow gap in the reef and heading straight for them.

It carried a crew of two, a boy and a girl. They looked like twins, about the same size as Sally. They had black hair and brown skin.

The cat had one big sail made of brightly colored strips. The name *Gemini* was painted in large letters on the outside of each of the two hulls.

Sally felt as though two strangers were forcing their way right into her living room. But she'd been polite. When they came whizzing past her and Andy in knee-deep water, she said, "Hi!"

They just glared at her. The boy raised a fist. "Go away!" he shouted. "That's *our* camping place. You be gettin' out of there!"

And then they were gone, speeding silently out of the lagoon toward the deep waters of the sound outside.

"No fair!" cried Andy, hopping awkwardly through the water after them. "We were here first!"

Sally just stood quite still, not knowing what to say or do. Her mouth was dry and she felt a little sick in the stomach. It was a while before she remembered to call Andy back into the shallow water. She hoped the twins wouldn't return.

But they did.

They came back the very next day, while Sally and her brothers were exploring the island and getting lost in the dense bush between Crusty Flats and the western shore.

When eventually they limped back to Fort Redwing, tired and thirsty, they found a note in a split stick planted in front of the tent. It said:

We are serious. You be getting out—or else.
Signed: the Geminis.

Sally shuddered as she thought about it. She wasn't afraid to fight for her rights, but there was something scary about this threat. And she had her brothers to look after. . . .

Peter was looking at her and pointing to the island. "Time to tack!" he cried. "We're nearly lined up with the gap in the reef."

"Lee-ho!" She pushed the tiller down and *Redwing* spun around smartly in a neat arc.

"Do you figure they're local people?" said Sally.

"Who?"

"The Geminis."

"I guess they must be. They look like Virgin Islanders."

"Then maybe they know we live on a yacht," said Sally. "Maybe they think they can frighten us into going back to *Freebooter*."

"I don't want to go back to *Freebooter* while Dad's away," said Peter.

"Neither do I."

Freebooter was the forty-five-foot sailboat they were helping Dad sail around the world. When Dad first learned that he had to go to New York, he'd made plans to moor *Freebooter* in front of the little hotel, two miles away on the other side of the island.

"She'll be safe here, Dr. Grant," the friendly hotel manager, Mr. Fred Whitely, had said. "We'll keep an eye on her while you're away. And the children, too, of course."

Sally snorted as she remembered his words. She was glad she'd persuaded Dad to let them camp at Fort Redwing instead. He'd agreed, on condition that if there was any trouble, they had to go back to *Freebooter* and Mr. Whitely. . . .

Peter was talking again. "One more tack," he said. "Just a little one."

Sally nodded. She had to get this one just right because the gap in the reef was only ten feet wide. *Redwing* was nearly five feet wide, so there wasn't much room to spare.

As they came about, Sally quickly hauled in the mainsail. Then she reached across Peter to pull in the jib.

"I can do it," he protested. "It's my job."

"It has to be done quickly this time."

"I know. I was going to do it quickly."

"Peter, don't argue."

He shrugged hopelessly and lapsed into silence.

They raced quickly through the narrow entrance of jagged coral like a cork popping out of a bottle. And then they were leaving a creamy, hissing wake in the still, turquoise green waters of the lagoon.

To Sally's relief, Andy came bounding down from Lookout Point to meet them. His skinny arms and legs made awkward angles as he leaped over crab holes in the pathway.

He reached the beach just before *Redwing* did and waded into the water to catch the bow.

He gave Sally a snappy naval salute. "Everything in order, skipper," he reported. "No enemy action. No sign of the cat."

"Good," said Sally. "Well done, ship's lookout."

"Did you use the engine?" he asked.

Redwing had a little outboard motor tilted up out of the water.

"Of course not," said Sally. Andy always asked that. He was crazy about engines. "We had a great sail, thanks. Didn't need the engine today."

Andy pulled a sad face. "What a waste," he said, patting the little 2½-horsepower motor affectionately.

All three of them dragged *Redwing* up the white, powdery beach. Sally carefully planted the anchor in the sand ahead of the bow so she wouldn't drift away at high tide.

They carried the flashlight batteries and fresh provisions to the campsite in the low trees just a few yards above the beach. There was no message on a stick this time. Sally was glad to see the tent was undisturbed.

She went back down to the beach to make sure Peter was furling the sails and coiling the ropes properly; and that was when she first heard the strange peep-peeping sound.

It seemed to come from nowhere and everywhere at the same time.

"Can you hear it?" she asked the others.

Peter nodded.

"Where's it coming from?"

Peter shrugged and shook his head.

It was the kind of squeak a newly hatched chicken might make, but higher and longer and squeakier. The air all around them seemed to be filled with the nervous, high-pitched noise. It wasn't loud but it wasn't difficult to hear, either. And it didn't stop.

Then, all at once, Andy yelled and galloped down to the water's edge in the far corner of the lagoon.

"Hey!" he shouted. "Look, look, come and look at this!"

Sally could hardly believe her eyes.

It was a dolphin, a sleek, black, fully grown dolphin.

And he was dying.

2

FIGHTING TALK

The dolphin lay in the shallows with only his back and head out of the water. The squeaky noises of pain and distress came from the breathing hole behind his head.

The water all around him glowed red. Deep cuts sliced his back open, running across at angles. Dark red blood oozed thickly from each one.

"He's been hit by a motorboat," gasped Sally. "He's been chopped up by a propeller."

She felt a flood of pity for the poor creature. She wished she could hug him and comfort him. He was lying so still. But he must be in terrible pain.

Peter ran down to see what they were looking at.

"Don't get too close," Sally warned. "We mustn't frighten him away."

"Okay, okay, take it easy," Peter grumbled. "I won't scare him."

"I know who did it!" Andy yelled. "I know who did it! I wrote it in the log. I know the name of the boat."

Peter said, "Did you see it happen?"

"I saw a boat stop near the gap into the lagoon. First it was going fast and then it stopped. There was a man and a woman." He turned to Sally. "You said I should write down anything suspicious, so I did. I thought they were spying on our camp."

"Did you see the dolphin?" asked Sally.

"No. I only saw the man go to the back of the boat and look over. Then I thought they must be having engine trouble," said Andy. "There was oil in the water behind them. At least, it looked like oil . . . only"—he paused—"perhaps it was blood."

"It must have been," said Peter, squatting down next to the dolphin and trying to judge the depth of the cuts. "And now he's drifted into the lagoon to die."

"No, no! We can't just let him die," said Sally desperately. "We've got to do something. I wish Dad was here."

Peter stood up slowly. "Let's go and look at the first-aid book," he suggested. "It might give us an idea."

Sally already knew some first aid. Dad had made sure of that. And even before she opened the first-aid book they kept in the plastic box in the tent, she was certain about two things.

First, the bleeding should be stopped. Second, the poor dolphin would be in a state of shock after the accident with the motorboat. And shock, she knew, was serious, even if it sometimes didn't *look* very alarming.

Peter stepped into the tent and sniffed at a tube of antiseptic ointment. "How about this?" he asked. "If we pressed some of this into his wounds it would stop the bleeding."

"No," said Sally, flipping through the book. The pages felt droopy and well worn. "The seawater would wash it right out. We need plastic dressings to close the wounds."

"Wouldn't work, either," said Andy, slipping in behind Peter. "His skin's wet. They wouldn't stick."

"Would, too, if you dried the skin first," Peter insisted.

"Cut it out, you two," said Sally. "I'm trying to read."

There on page 74, under the heading "Treatment for Shock," she found the information she wanted: "Keep patient warm. Keep patient still. No food should be given to the patient. Every effort should be made to stop loss of blood. Immediate hospital attention is vital."

Peter peeked over her shoulder. "I guess the first three are easy. He's in warm water. He's keeping still. And he can't hunt for food."

"But we've still got to stop the bleeding," said Sally urgently.

She picked up a packet of plastic wound dressings and threw it back hopelessly. "Too small," she said, "and there aren't enough, anyway."

Peter scratched his head slowly, as he so often did when he was thinking. "What about duct tape?" he said. "Same stuff, really."

"Duct tape?" Sally couldn't remember what it was for a moment.

"It's that wide plastic tape in *Freebooter*'s toolbox," said Peter.

"The really sticky stuff we use to seal the hatches at sea?"

"Yeah, that's it. I bet it'll stick better than these silly little things."

It was worth a try. Better than doing nothing.

"I'll grab it for you," said Andy quickly, hopping on one leg. "I know where it is. I'll take *Redwing*. I'll use the motor."

"No you don't," said Sally sternly. "You stay right here. You're not allowed to take *Redwing* out alone until you can swim. You know that. Peter, you fetch the duct tape, please. And get back here as fast as you can."

"No fair!" said Andy, hopping some more. "I asked first. I should be the one to go!"

"Andy! Now quit it, will you?"

They all helped pull *Redwing* into the water. Peter started the motor and steered for the lagoon entrance. Little exhaust bubbles popped blue smoke in *Redwing*'s white wake. Andy watched enviously.

"C'mon," said Sally, dragging him away along the warm white sand. "Let's see if we can make friends with the dolphin."

They crept up to him very slowly and he didn't move. Perhaps he was too weak. Sally put out a hand to touch him on the back of his head, where there were no cuts. She did it very slowly, just to see if he would do anything.

"It's okay," said Andy confidently, "dolphins don't bite."

"What do you know? How do they catch fish, then?"

For once, Andy was at a loss for words.

But the dolphin stayed very still and let Sally stroke him. His black skin was soft and cool. It felt just like a tractor inner tube she used to swim with, springy but tight. Her fingers formed little dimples in his flesh.

His squeaky voice fell silent now as little wavelets

lapped the white sand around him. Once every minute or so he opened his breathing valve and expelled air in a long sigh.

His sad, deep-brown eyes glinted moistly. He stared at Sally without blinking.

"He knows we're trying to help him," Sally whispered.

Andy lowered himself in the water beside him and covered him with little pats. "Don't die, Mr. Dolphin," he said quietly. "Please don't die."

Peter returned within a half hour with the big roll of silver duct tape. Sally hacked off twelve-inch lengths of the wide tape with her sailing knife.

Peter dried the dolphin's skin with a clean towel and squeezed the edges of the wounds together while Sally pressed the tape firmly on top.

One by one, the six big wounds stopped bleeding. The murky red water around the dolphin slowly turned clear again. Only once did the dolphin show any sign of pain or discomfort. That was when Peter closed the gap in the first wound, and the dolphin made a halfhearted effort to wriggle back into deeper water.

After that he lay perfectly still. He knew they were trying to help.

When they were finished they gingerly caught

hold of his tail and dragged him back into deeper water to keep his skin wet. Only his head, with its blowhole, stuck out.

Sally flopped down onto the soft sand of the beach. She felt tired, but happy that they'd been able to help. It was late afternoon, and the low sun glistened red and gold on the dolphin's head with every slight movement he made.

"He looks like a package that came to pieces in the mail and had to be strapped together again," said Peter. He chuckled at his own wit. Then, after a bit, he added gravely: "What happens if he swims away during the night?"

Sally didn't think he would. "He's very weak," she pointed out. "And besides, he deliberately came in to the beach so he wouldn't have to keep swimming."

"Yeah, I guess that makes sense," said Peter, breaking into a slow, wide grin. "Sometimes, just sometimes, my big sister does make sense."

She grabbed the bloodstained towel and threw it at him indignantly. But deep down inside she felt quite pleased. It was nice when he let her know he liked her. It was nice when Peter wasn't sulking and Andy wasn't fighting with her.

"Maybe we should tie a noose over his tail," said Andy. "Just to be safe."

"No, I'll tell you what," said Sally. "We'll keep watch over him tonight. He won't go away if we keep showing him we want to help. He needs someone to sit up with him tonight and stroke him and talk to him now and then. How about that?"

"Great!" said Andy, "I'll do it, I'll do it!"

"We'll all take turns," said Sally. She picked up the towel and rinsed it out in the warm, shallow water. "We'll set proper watches, just like we do when *Freebooter*'s at sea."

"Sounds good to me," said Peter.

"And me," said Andy.

Sally stood up to go back to the camp. "That's settled, then. I'll take the first—" She stopped in midsentence.

Skimming along stealthily just outside their reef was a catamaran with a brightly colored sail. She felt her heart pounding.

"We'd better get back to the tent," she said.

She forced herself to move quite slowly, to stroll almost, as if she hadn't noticed *Gemini* racing in through the gap. She didn't want anyone to think she was scared.

By the time the catamaran ran her shallow hulls up on the beach, the defenders of Fort Redwing were lined up in front of their camp.

The twins wore peaked caps over their black

hair. The girl took her cap off and pushed her dark sunglasses up onto her head with an arrogant gesture. On a cord around her neck she wore a watch with big numbers. Her left wrist rustled with a bracelet of seashells.

The boy wore a diver's knife in a black sheath hanging from his belt.

The girl jumped ashore, pointed excitedly, and said, "Look, see what they've done! They've killed a dolphin!"

Sally felt her face flush. But she said nothing. As the twins came up the beach she edged forward to meet them, leaving Peter and Andy standing in front of the tent.

The twins slowed down as they drew nearer, keeping close together. Sally slowed down, too, but she wouldn't stop. Neither would the twins. They kept coming slowly, relentlessly, toward her. They stared into each other's eyes.

Finally, when there were just a few feet separating them, Sally drew a line in the sand with the toe of her sneaker. She didn't know what made her do it. It was as if her foot were acting all on its own. The sun went behind a cloud and she felt a sudden cold shadow on her back. She went over the line several times, slowly and deliberately, digging it wider and deeper.

She halted right there behind the line. The twins continued to move toward her, closer and closer. She clenched her hands. The palms were wet and slippery. She could feel them with her fingertips.

The twins came right up to the line and stopped. They stood face-to-face.

"We didn't kill him," said Sally evenly. "That's not fair. We're trying to save him. He's badly injured. But he's alive and we're trying to help."

The girl twin shrugged as if it didn't really matter, anyway. "We told you to get out of our camp," she said. "Why are you still here?"

Her brother tugged her gently by the elbow. "Whoa," he said, "let's be doing this thing proper, like." He looked Sally straight in the eye. He spoke slowly and clearly, with a Caribbean lilt.

"Our names are Jon and Jan Selby. We live away across the sound, in Hurricane Haven, oh, maybe three miles from here."

"And you've got to get out!" said Jan, waving her arms. "You shouldn't still be here."

"Wait, bide your time now," said her brother. He looked at Sally. "Every year we camp here during the holidays. It's our camp, you see."

Sally looked down at her feet uncertainly. "Your camp?"

Jan stepped forward, right up to the very edge

of the line in the sand. "Yes, our camp," she said, putting her nose almost up against Sally's. "We cut back the bush and made a level place for the tent."

"We've camped here every year for three years," said Jon. "We built the fireplace. We cleared the path to Spyglass Hill."

"To where?" said Sally.

Jan pointed to Lookout Point. "See," she said triumphantly, "you don't even know the proper names." She put her hands on her hips. "You better be getting yourselves out of here, or else . . ."

"But we got here first," Sally protested. "And this isn't the only campsite. There's another one just around the corner."

"It's full of mosquitoes," said Jon. "Big fellers."

"And crabs," said Jan.

"And there's no gap in the reef."

"So we can't get our boat in or out, except at high tide."

"But in any case," said Jon flatly, "this is our camp and we want it back. If you folks want to camp, then *you* can be going to the other place."

"What if we don't go?" It was a hard question to ask, but Sally wanted to know the worst.

The twins looked at each other. "Oh, things can happen," said Jon darkly. "You know, accidents, like."

"Tents can be falling down," Jan hinted. "Boats can be getting holes in them. Things like that."

"You wouldn't dare!" said Sally. She whirled around and pointed at her brothers. "There are three of us."

Jon's lips parted in a thin smile that showed a slit of white teeth against his brown skin. He plainly didn't think Sally and her brothers were a match for the two of them. "You just wait and see," he said softly.

"But it isn't fair to make us leave without notice."

"You can have one more day. That's all." Jon shook his head. "Don't talk about fair. You had notice twice already."

"But we've got to get the dolphin to a hospital. We'll need at least a day for that."

"Hospital?" said Jon in astonishment. "You mean human hospital?"

"Yes. He's a mammal, just like us."

"Hospital?" He shook his head. "Down Tortuga way?"

"Yes," said Sally, a little uncertainly. "That's the nearest one isn't it?"

Jan laughed at Sally's ignorance. "That's the *only* one," she said. "But how will you get him there? That thing be weighing as much as two full-grown men, don't you know?"

Jon said: "You can't take him in your little boat. Not that big feller. Not enough room. You won't be able to move."

"We have a plan," said Sally. She put her hands behind her back and crossed her fingers. She looked down and made the line in the sand a little deeper with her toe.

"All right," said Jon eventually. "We mean no harm to your dolphin. Island people are reasonable people. You can have one extra day."

"Two more days altogether," said Jan with great finality. "That's all. Definitely all. Then you be clearing out."

She put on her sunglasses and tucked their red string down the back of her collar. "Let's go," she said to Jon.

They stepped two paces backward, away from the line in the sand, not taking their eyes off Sally. Then they turned around and sauntered casually to their boat.

Peter and Andy came to stand on either side of Sally at the line in the sand. They watched in silence while the twins readied their boat.

None of them liked catamarans. Show-off boats, Peter called them. They were fast all right, but they were sort of clumsy.

Sally knew their twin hulls made them slow to

turn. Not like *Redwing*. *Redwing* was so agile and easy to turn she could spin around on a dime. Dad said Hobie cats were Californian surfboats. "Lots of fun at the beach, but not boats for serious sailors like us."

Even so, it was plain to Sally that *Gemini*'s crew knew how to sail. *Gemini* was much wider than *Redwing* and she was going much faster when she whizzed out through the gap in the reef with only inches to spare. Jon and Jan didn't look back.

"Okay, stop staring now," said Sally. "Time to cook supper before it gets dark. Andy, did you collect firewood?"

"Yup."

"Good. Go and make the fire."

"Peter—you peel the potatoes. I'll fetch some more water."

Sally suddenly felt the need for some action after the meeting with the Geminis. The walk to the freshwater spring on the way to Lookout Point would calm her down a bit.

And maybe, if she concentrated hard, she'd *really* think of a plan to get the dolphin to the hospital.

3

PROBLEMS AT THE HOSPITAL

There was a glimmer of an idea in Sally's mind already about how to get the dolphin to the hospital, as a matter of fact.

As she walked back along the sandy path to the camp, with two plastic jerricans filled with fresh spring water, she felt quite sure they could tow him to Mission Harbor behind *Redwing*. She just didn't know quite how. But she was certain that was the way real sailors would do it.

Andy came skipping along the path to meet her. "Fire's going great guns," he announced cheerfully.

"You're crazy about fires," said Sally.

"It's my job."

"I know, and if I wasn't here you'd burn the island down."

"I wouldn't, I wouldn't, I'm real careful." He

jumped over a large crab hole and landed with one foot each side of another hole. Then he said, "Do we really have to leave here after two days and go back to *Freebooter*?"

"Yes," said Sally. "I agreed."

"Aren't we even going to fight? It isn't fair to kick us out when we got here first. They don't own the island."

"We can't fight them *and* get the dolphin to the hospital," said Sally. "You know he needs to be stitched up. Maybe they'll give him some injections, too. He's dying and we have to save him. His life must come first." She stopped and put down the cans for a moment to give her arms a rest. "C'mon Andy, at least we've got to try."

"Well, okay," he said. "I just wish we could have fires on *Freebooter*, that's all."

Sally laughed. "Back to camp!" she said, picking up the cans. "Go tend your fire while you can. And I hope you've got a lot of wood, because we're going to keep it going all night long."

"Yea!" cried Andy, dashing off ahead of her. "I get to stay up all night."

"Oh no you don't!" said Sally. But it was no good. He was out of hearing range already. She sighed. Trying to control Andy was like trying to calm a whirlwind.

*   *   *

After supper, when they were all washing the dishes in the little aluminum basin, Peter said to Sally, "Do you really have a plan to get the dolphin to the hospital? Or did you just say that because the Geminis were here?"

"Well"—Sally hesitated—"I *sort of* have a plan. I, um, I think we should tow him behind *Redwing*."

"You mean, tie a rope around him and pull him through the water?"

"Sort of."

Peter reached around and scratched his shoulder blade absentmindedly with a fork. "It would have to be tied around his tail," he said, "otherwise it would slip off."

"But you can't tow him backward," said Andy. "He'll drown."

Sally looked at Peter. "Is that true?" she asked. "You're the fisherman."

"No, he's got it wrong," said Peter. "It's fish that drown when you tow them. But a dolphin has a blowhole on the back of his head to breathe through."

"That's right," said Sally. "But towing him backward worries me. He might not be able to balance. He has to keep his blowhole on top so he can breathe."

"So okay, put him in a bag and tow him forward," said Peter.

"A bag?"

"Sure. How about our tent bag? It's big enough."

"Okay . . . ," said Sally slowly. She was trying to imagine how it would look. "But we'd need to make a hole in the bag for him to breathe through."

"I can do it," said Andy. "My knife is good for that."

"We'll see," she said. "Let's get finished here first."

She felt relieved that they had a plan. Putting the dolphin in a bag would also make it easier to carry him from the water to the hospital.

It wasn't far, she knew, because she'd seen the hospital when they were shopping in Mission Harbor yesterday. But they would need help. And it would be almost impossible to carry a heavy, slippery dolphin unless he was in a bag.

"Just one more thing," she said. "Who will come with me? I don't trust those Geminis. Someone ought to stay here and guard the camp again."

"I'll stay," said Peter. "I want to do some fishing from the rocks."

"Well, that's decided then," she announced. "We'll do it first thing in the morning."

"I'm going to get my book of knots and find one

for tying a dolphin to a boat," said Andy, disappearing into the tent.

"And I'm going to feed the ginger beer plant," said Peter.

Sally felt a twinge of guilt about that. It wasn't really a plant, of course, just some water in a jam jar with a loose lid. It had yeast in it, and every day Peter added some ground ginger and a spoon of sugar.

It was fun to watch the yeast burp after it had eaten the sugar. It made big explosions in the muddy ginger powder at the bottom.

At the end of each week, except when *Freebooter* was at sea, Peter strained the plant, mixed it with water, and made twelve bottles of ginger beer.

It was really Sally's job, but she'd made a mess of it. For some reason she'd kept putting in too much sugar. That made the bottles explode.

Dad had asked her to hand over the job to Peter after one really bad explosion in a cupboard at home. The first bottle had exploded at 2:00 A.M. like a rifle going off. Then, all the other bottles had started exploding, too.

The flying glass ripped some flour bags to shreds and shattered bottles of cooking oil. When they all came downstairs in their robes, wide-eyed with alarm, a sticky river of ginger beer, flour, and cooking oil was flowing over the kitchen floor. Razor-sharp shards of glass lined the wooden shelves and the cupboard doors. Dad said it was lucky nobody was near when the ginger beer bomb went off, otherwise he might have lost an eye or a leg.

Sally felt really bad about that. Except at school, of course. When her friends heard about it she became quite famous. The science teacher worked out that the pressure inside the ginger beer bottles was greater than that inside a truck tire.

She was lucky Peter didn't mind taking over her duty. In the first place, he quite liked cooking and things like that. It sort of went with his big love, which was fishing. And in the second place, he had confided to Sally, it gave him power over Andy. Everybody knew Andy would do almost anything for a homemade ginger beer.

Sally was a bit sorry now that *she'd* lost that power over Andy. There were times when the promise of a bottle of ginger beer might have helped her to keep him under control. Still, she didn't have time to worry about it now. It was getting dark. It was time to start the dolphin watches.

She took the first watch as soon as the others were tucked up in their sleeping bags inside the tent.

Although the wind had died down and the night was warm, Sally took a sweater down to the beach with her. She knew it would get cold later on.

She waded into the shallow water and stroked the dolphin's head. He lay very still and didn't make any noise, but every now and then he wiggled his flippers gently as if to say he liked to be stroked.

When he opened his blowhole it was surprisingly loud and sudden in the quiet night air. She smelled the warm, humid mustiness of his breath.

Little waves in the lagoon had washed some sand away from under him, so he was resting in a little hollow the shape of his body. His very own water bed, thought Sally.

She put her face close to his. "I'm not going away," she whispered. "I'll be right here on the beach."

In the background, the low light of the campfire flickered comfortingly on the front of the tent. Andy had wanted to make a fire on the beach where they were going to sit, close by the dolphin, but Sally was afraid it would upset him. Now she was glad to know the dolphin could see the fire from where he was.

Sally wrapped her arms around her knees and gazed out over the black sea to where the lights of Tortuga and Mission Harbor shone dimly but steadily. At the entrance to the harbor a lighthouse swung its beam over the water every ten seconds and flashed brightly.

She lay back and let the lingering warmth of the sand seep through her shirt. It would get cold pretty soon. On top, anyway. If you dug deeper down it would still be warm for most of the night.

Straight over her head, hundreds of stars winked at her, cold and distant. Every now and then, puffs of wind formed little cat's-paws on the calm surface of the lagoon and raced toward the reef. High overhead, the breeze rattled the palm trees that divided the beach from the bush.

Once in a while, a large fish leaped out of the water and fell back with a plop that startled her. Small, dark birds made quick, darting flights in complete silence. The ocean swells slurped and sucked greedily at the edges of the reefs.

When the wind made goose bumps on her arms she pulled on her sweater and went to stroke the dolphin some more, using the flat of her hand, gently dragging her palm across his soft, wet skin.

And then, when it was Peter's turn to take over the watch, she knelt in the water beside the dolphin and gave him a soft hug.

Peter was sleepy-eyed and only half-awake, so she stayed with him for a while.

"What were you and Andy talking about before you went to sleep?" she asked.

Peter yawned widely. "Names," he said. "I thought we should have a name for ourselves. Something like theirs."

"Whose?"

"The Geminis'."

"It's just the name of their boat."

"I know, but it sounds good."

"Well, how about the Redwings then?" Sally thought that was logical enough.

"We shouldn't be copycats," said Peter. "That's just the name of *our* boat." He paused. "I thought of the Piscators." He waited for some sign of approval.

"The Piscators?"

"Yes. It's a Latin word," he said defensively. "A good, strong, Latin word. It means fishermen."

"Hmm," said Sally. "And what did Andy suggest?"

"The Turk's Heads."

"What the heck is that?"

"Some ancient knot he found in his book. He's been practicing. Says it's magic."

"I don't like that name."

"Neither do I, but you know what Andy's like."

"We'll think about it," said Sally. "I'm sure we can do better than that. Are you awake enough now?"

"I guess so."

"Be sure to take good care of him."

"I will."

Sally went over to kiss the dolphin good night. But she didn't think she should put her lips to his skin. She kissed her hand and pressed it gently on top of his head.

She ruffled Peter's hair as she went past. "Tell Andy to wake me ten minutes before my next watch starts. I'm going to get some sleep now."

"Okay. G'night."

Next morning, as soon as the gray, predawn light crept in from the east, they ate breakfast and got *Redwing* ready. They fetched the tent bag and slipped it up over the dolphin's tail. They found they didn't need to cut a hole in it after all. It was shorter than they thought and the dolphin's head stuck out.

Peter took a long, critical look. "No problem," he said at last. "Now he can breathe."

Andy tied the bag to the boat with two lines to keep it upright, and they were ready.

Peter gave the dolphin a farewell pat.

"We won't be late," said Sally. "We'll set him free in Mission Harbor as soon as he's stitched up properly. We'll be back before dark."

The morning trade wind was light but fair. *Redwing*'s mainsail and jib swelled gently, one either side of the mast, as they ran downwind toward the island of Tortuga.

The little dinghy, and the precious cargo she had in tow, slipped quietly through the smooth, deep water, rising and falling gently to the swells moving up lazily from astern.

"How fast are we going?" asked Andy.

"Oh, three or four knots," said Sally, who was steering. "It's kind of slow because of the dolphin. Are there any ships about?"

Andy sat at the forward end of the cockpit, where he could see under the jib. He was the lookout.

"No ships so far," he said. He closed his eyes tightly.

"You're not going to sleep, are you?"

"No, I'm thinking."

"Of what?"

"A name for the dolphin."

Sally looked back behind *Redwing*. The tent bag was towing very nicely, making two big ripples in the water. The dolphin was breathing regularly and keeping very still. "It should begin with a *d*," she said.

"I know that. I thought of Donald and Dick already," said Andy, taking a quick look under the jib. "But Donald sounds like a duck and Dick is really short for Richard."

"Dennis," said Sally. "How about Dennis?"

Andy shook his head vigorously. "It's not Ella Quint enough," he said.

"Not *what*?"

"Not Ella Quint enough."

"Who's she?"

"I don't know. That's what Peter said about my name for us—Turk's Heads."

"Do you mean 'eloquent'?"

"No. Peter said Ella Quint. Well . . ." Suddenly he was unsure. "Maybe," he added reluctantly. At that moment he luckily spotted a schooner leaving Mission Harbor. "Sail ho!" he cried hurriedly. "On the port bow."

"I have her," said Sally. "Thank you, lookout."

The towlines dipped into the swells and sprayed droplets as they pulled taut. The wind was waking up after a lazy start to the day. Now it was trying out some fresher puffs. *Redwing* scudded along before them.

"Daniel!" Andy said suddenly.

"What's that?"

"Daniel."

"Daniel Quint?"

"No, silly!" Andy pulled a face at her. "Daniel Dolphin. I was thinking about him coming into the lion's den."

"You mean the lagoon? That doesn't make much sense. No lions in there."

"I know, I know, it was just the first part of my thought," Andy grumbled. "Then, the second part of my thought was: Daniel is a good name for a dolphin."

"Not bad," said Sally. "Quite dignified, I guess. Quite Ella Quint." She chuckled and Andy looked at her suspiciously.

"Do you really like it?"

"Yes," she said, "you'd better christen him."

Andy scrambled back and crouched in the stern. "I christen thee Daniel Dolphin," he said. Daniel gazed back at him with soft dark eyes.

"You should pour some champagne over his head," said Sally, "like they do when they're naming a ship."

"I wish we had some ginger beer," said Andy. "If he's got any sense he'd rather have ginger beer."

Two hours after they had set sail from Fort Redwing, Sally and Andy beached the boat on a sandy spit near Mission Harbor's main commercial jetty, where the interisland ferries tied up.

The hospital lay just across the road. Its glass doors slid open automatically as they approached.

Inside, a woman in a stiff white uniform sat behind a desk. "Yes?" she asked. "What is it?"

Sally said, "We need help."

"For whom?"

"For our dolphin. He's on the beach. He's badly hurt and in shock."

The woman sniffed loudly. "A dolphin?" she said. "Now really! Please don't waste my time. This is a hospital. You can't bring a dirty old fish in here."

4

REDWING RUNS INTO TROUBLE

Sally stared at the woman behind the counter. She felt her heart pounding. Her hands forced themselves into tight fists at her sides.

"He's not a fish. He's a dolphin, a mammal like you and me."

"My dear girl, it makes no difference. This is a hospital for humans. A dolphin in a hospital? I've never heard of such a thing."

"We'd like to see a doctor, please."

"They're all busy."

"But this is an emergency. He's dying."

"I'm sorry, but it's quite impossible . . ."

Sally gripped the edge of the counter tightly. "We *must* see a doctor," she said. And after a moment's pause she added desperately: "If you don't

41

fetch a doctor we're just going to . . . we're going to . . ."

". . . stand here and scream for help," said Andy.

"Good idea!" yelled Sally enthusiastically.

Andy tried an experimental shout: "Help!"

"Louder," said Sally. "Both together. *Help—help—help—help!*"

A tall, gray-haired man pushed hurriedly through the swing doors at the back of the room. He wore a long white jacket, and a stethoscope flopped around his neck. His glasses perched at the end of his nose.

"What's going on?" he said sternly, creasing his brow in puzzlement at the scene before him.

"Oh, Dr. Watkins," said the nurse.

Sally interrupted her. "Please, we need your help."

She explained about the dolphin's accident and how they had patched up his wounds. "He's not far away, please come and look at him."

Dr. Watkins peered at her dubiously over the top of his glasses. "I'm not sure that—"

"Please, it won't take a minute."

"Just tell us what to do," said Andy.

"He'll die if you don't."

"It's just across the road."

Dr. Watkins shrugged helplessly. "Nurse Jenkins," he said, "I'm going to the beach for a moment."

The end of Nurse Jenkins's long thin nose twitched sideways as she gave a little sniff. She kept writing in her book.

Andy undid the towlines and tugged Daniel up to the beach. Dr. Watkins peeled the bag back and placed his stethoscope on the dolphin's skin.

"Well, I never," he said, puzzling over the patchwork quilt of silvery plastic tape on the dark skin. "It's unusual—but you've done quite well."

"My father is a doctor, and I want to be one, too," Sally explained. She told him their names. Dr. Watkins listened to the stethoscope.

"Well, you're right," he said. "He needs stitches and treatment for severe shock. We must get help to carry him across the road."

Sally grinned. Andy did a triumphant little war dance.

Back at the hospital, Dr. Watkins faced the woman behind the counter. "Nurse Jenkins, order a gurney immediately. And six bearers. It's a very heavy load."

She closed her jaw in a hard line and hesitated.

"If you please, Nurse," he insisted.

"Well, sir, it's highly unusual."

"I'll take the responsibility, Nurse Jenkins."

He turned to Sally. "Did you say your name is

Grant? Is your father Dr. Harold Phillip Grant, the heart surgeon?"

"Yes."

"Well, isn't that strange? Only last month I was reading a paper he wrote for a medical journal." He shook her hand formally. "I'll tell you what. I want you to be my helper. We're going to give your friend an injection of antibiotics and we're going to stitch him up."

Sally felt like doing a cartwheel right in front of everybody. But with Nurse Jenkins looking on, she decided it would be better to behave like a lady.

"Why certainly, Dr. Watkins," she said. "I'd be pleased to assist." And when the nurse wasn't looking she turned and gave Andy a big wink.

They walked to the air-conditioned waiting room. Sally watched in awe as six men wheeled Daniel in, tent bag and all, and disappeared in the direction of the operating theater.

"Come along then," Dr. Watkins said. "Let's get scrubbed up. We'll find you a mask and a gown."

"Be good," Sally said to Andy. "I won't be long."

"It's okay," said Andy, fishing out a length of string. "I'm going to practice Turk's heads."

The moment she entered the operating theater Sally felt very nervous. To tell the truth, she had no idea what to do. She was afraid Dr. Watkins had got the wrong idea. She was scared of doing something that might make the dolphin worse.

The room was dark at the edges but Daniel's skin sparkled in the bright light from the overhead fittings in the center. The air was filled with strange smells of medicines and antiseptics.

But the doctor was very nice. "Just do what I tell you," he said, "and—here's the golden rule—ask if you need to know something."

She helped him slip the tent bag under Daniel's stocky body. He started to examine the dolphin more carefully. Then he paused. "What did you say the dolphin is called?"

"Daniel."

"That's a male name, isn't it?"

"Yes," said Sally.

He laughed. "I've got news for you," he said. "This dolphin is a female."

"A female?" Sally bit her lip. That was a silly mistake for a doctor's daughter. Everybody had just assumed it was a male.

"Yes. No doubt about it." Dr. Watkins ran his hands over the dolphin's body, pressing here and prodding there. "I can tell you something else," he said. "She's pregnant. She's going to have a baby—and pretty soon, I'd say. Can you look after her for a while? Keep her quiet somewhere for a few days until she's over the shock of the accident?"

Sally hadn't bargained for that. Somehow she had just imagined they would free Daniel in the waters of the harbor after he—she—had been treated at the hospital.

"I expect we could keep her in our little lagoon," she said. "It's warm and calm."

"Sounds just right. You'll have to feed her, of course. Can you catch fish?"

"My brother Peter can."

"Well, that's all right then."

The operation was over surprisingly quickly. Sally did just what Dr. Watkins told her. Mostly she handed him the instruments he pointed at. She cut the ends off the stitches and dabbed antiseptic on the wounds.

Only twenty minutes after she had been taken into the theater, the dolphin was wheeled out again on the gurney. Dr. Watkins had sewn up the cuts with twenty-four large stitches, four in each cut.

The gut he used for the stitches was a special kind that slowly dissolved in the skin. It would take ten days to disappear. During that time the skin would grow together again.

Dr. Watkins had given Daniel two injections, an antibiotic to kill germs while the wounds were healing and another to take away the pain and keep him—or, rather, her—quiet during the long journey back to the lagoon.

They slipped the damp tent bag over her tail and pulled it up as far as it would go. "That's good," said Dr. Watkins. "Don't let the skin dry out."

But when the helpers were ready to leave with Daniel, Nurse Jenkins tapped her pen noisily on the desk and said: "Who's going to pay?"

"Pay?" said Sally, walking toward the desk. She hadn't given a thought to paying.

Nurse Jenkins had a look of triumph on her face. "No patient may leave the hospital unless arrangements have been made to pay the bill," she announced. She looked at Dr. Watkins. "It's hospital rules."

"Absolutely right, Nurse," he said. "But we mustn't be too hasty. We haven't yet received Miss Grant's bill."

Sally halted in surprise. But it was nothing compared with the look on Nurse Jenkins's face. "Bill?" she said. "Her *bill*?"

"Why, yes," said Dr. Watkins smoothly. "I engaged her to help me with the operation. As the daughter of a famous surgeon, she is well qualified. And as you know, it's hard to find good help in the islands."

Nurse Jenkins pulled her white cap down more tightly on her hair and pursed her lips disapprovingly.

Dr. Watkins said, "What happens if Sally's bill—

ah, that is, Miss Grant's bill—is bigger than ours, Nurse? We'd owe her money, then, wouldn't we?"

"Well, yes, but . . ." Nurse Jenkins looked as though she were going to say, "How silly!" But she wisely held her tongue.

Dr. Watkins said, "It's quite easy, really. If Miss Grant will agree, I propose that she charge the hospital exactly the same amount that the hospital charges her." He looked at Sally. "What do you say to that?"

There was only one thing she could say. "I agree."

"Well that's that, then. The bills cancel each other out. We shan't have to pay her anything after all, Nurse Jenkins. Isn't that a stroke of luck?"

She shot him one of her sternest glares. "It also means *they* don't have to pay anything," she pointed out.

"Precisely," said Dr. Watkins.

He shook hands with Sally and Andy.

Sally said, "Thank you for all you've done."

"My pleasure," said Dr. Watkins smiling. "I haven't treated such an interesting case since I was at medical school and they brought in a circus elephant that got drunk on a barrel of rum." He looked at Daniel thoughtfully. "I wonder if the medical journal has ever published a paper about operating on dolphins . . . ?"

*　　*　　*

The going was easy at first. They crossed the road that ran around the perimeter of the island and then they joggled down the grassy embankment to the bay. There the gurney's wheels got stuck in the sand, so the bearers had to grab the tent bag and carry Daniel to the water.

Sally thanked the bearers and they turned away to go back to the hospital.

Andy said, "Don't they want to see the fun?"

"There won't be any fun," she said. "We're not releasing her. We're taking her back again. We have to look after her."

Andy spun around. "Her?" he cried. "Did you say *her*?"

Sally nodded. "And Dr. Watkins says she's pregnant."

Andy slapped his forehead and groaned. "Oh no!" he cried. "I'll have to think of a new name. Daniel's no good for a girl."

Andy tied the bag in place again, as he had done that morning. Only this time, with a dolphin who was pregnant as well as wounded and shocked, he was even more careful to tie the knots tightly.

When they were ready to go, Sally hoisted *Redwing*'s sails and lowered the heavy metal centerboard.

Once again, the dolphin followed obediently at

the end of the towline, but this time the going was not so good. That morning, the wind had been behind them. Now they had to beat against it, which was much slower; and they had farther to go because of the zigzags they had to make.

The wet tow ropes snapped taut and shed droplets like a dog shaking its coat every time *Redwing* plunged into a wave. Spray flew away from the bow in white plumes.

Sally realized they weren't making much headway. For a whole hour, *Redwing* had zigged and zagged toward home, first on port tack and then on starboard, plunging and rearing like a cart horse with an extraheavy load. But in all that time they had gained only about one mile to windward, in a straight line to the island.

Sally thought hard. They had five miles to go. That would take a further five hours. That was too long. That would make it eight o'clock. And it got dark at seven.

They wouldn't be able to find the gap in the reef in the dark. And in any case, Daniel's injection would keep her quiet for only a few more hours, Dr. Watkins had said.

Sally sighed deeply. She hadn't thought this out too well. If *Redwing* weren't towing the dolphin, they'd be home well before dark. But towing was a desperately slow business.

"We'll have to motor," she said. "Andy, come and start your pesky engine."

"Can't," he said. "The propeller will cut the towlines."

Her heart sank. How could she be so stupid? Here was the ship's lookout telling her how dumb she was.

"Okay," she said quietly. "We'll just sail on."

When darkness fell, *Redwing* was still a mile away from the lagoon. Sally felt tired, hungry, and despondent. Her arm muscles ached from pulling on the tiller.

There were no lights on this side of Crab Island. There was no moon, either. She couldn't see the reef, let alone the gap. She had no idea how they were going to find their way into the lagoon.

"We may be stuck out here all night," Sally warned.

"But what about Daniel?" said Andy. "Will she struggle and try to escape when the injection wears off?"

"I don't know. I just don't know."

At that moment Sally was close to tears.

5

DANIEL'S SURPRISE

As they plunged on into the darkness Sally could tell they were getting near the island. The land sheltered them from the wind. The waves were getting smaller, too.

It was dangerous to sail too close to the reef in the dark, but perhaps, now that it was calmer, if they went very slowly . . .

"Light dead ahead!" yelled Andy.

Sally understood as soon as she spotted the first leaping sparks. "Good old Peter!" she said. "He's building up the campfire to guide us home."

She suddenly felt all her muscles go limp with relief.

Daniel's injection must have worn off by now, but she was still keeping quiet. Now they had a chance to get her back into the lagoon in time.

"Get the flashlight out of the locker," Sally said. "Keep shining it at land, so Peter knows where we are. He's going to have to tell us when to tack." Only he could guide them in.

Sally sailed with all her skill in the dying wind, judging its direction by the feel of it against her cheek and the way it ruffled her hair.

Peter had seen their flashlight. Now he was shining his. "He's flashing," said Andy. "Dit-dah-dit-dit."

Morse code. Just like Dad had taught her. "That's *l*," said Sally. "He wants us to turn left. Ready about! Lee ho!"

Redwing tacked smartly, then angled in slowly toward the reef they couldn't see. It felt very strange, like a blind person being guided by a dog.

"Dit-dah-dit," said Andy.

"That's *r*. Ready about again . . ."

As they neared the gap, Peter made them sail in shorter tacks. Sally could see the fire better now. Shadows jumped on the walls of the tent. They must be getting close.

Suddenly Andy's voice was shouting: "Reef ahead!"

Sally yelled: "Are we okay? Are we heading for the gap?"

"Yes, keep going straight!"

Straight? That didn't sound correct. Surely the

gap was off to the right? Andy must be mixed up. He was guiding them onto the sharp coral reef.

She turned *Redwing* toward the right, where the gap should be.

"No, no!" yelled Andy. "Turn back the other way!" He pointed the flashlight ahead. It shone on unbroken reef. It was close now. In the pitch blackness *Redwing* seemed to be moving very fast.

Andy yelled desperately: "Turn left, turn left!"

At the last moment she thrust the tiller down and *Redwing* spun to the left. They scraped past a coral ledge with inches to spare, and, before she knew it, *Redwing* was dashing through the entrance gap.

"Straight now!" cried Andy. "Keep straight!"

Peter came running to meet them.

"Are you all right?"

"Yes, we're fine." Sally hopped out of the boat. Her legs felt shaky. "It's a good thing *Redwing* turns quickly," she said, "otherwise we'd have hit the reef."

Peter asked, "Why are you dragging the tent bag?"

"Daniel's in it. It's a long story," Sally replied.

"We've got a lot to tell you," said Andy.

"And I've got something to tell *you*," echoed Peter.

"Well, let's get Daniel settled first," said Sally, "then we can talk our heads off."

They towed Daniel to her old place in the shallows and pulled the bag off.

"He sure looks a lot more normal without the duct tape," observed Peter.

"She," said Andy.

"What?"

"It's a she," said Sally. "And she's going to have a baby."

"Wow! Is that why you brought her back?"

"Yes. And that's why we took so long."

Sally stroked Daniel's head, digging her fingers into the soft flesh and dragging them back. She traced the edges of a dark patch on her side that looked like a horse's saddle.

Daniel seemed to be quite happy to be in her old place once more. She looked tired after the long journey. But she was breathing regularly and her eyes looked bright.

"It's a good thing she didn't struggle on the way back," said Andy.

"I think she trusts us," said Sally. "She knows we're trying to help." She gave Daniel a pat. "Now you just have a good night's rest and we'll see you in the morning. Tomorrow you can have some food."

"I'll catch her some fish," said Peter. "I know a good spot . . . but will she stay in the lagoon tonight? Won't she swim away?"

"I don't think so," Sally answered. "She's exhausted. And she knows we're her friends. When she has her baby we'll fetch some netting from *Freebooter* and sling it across the lagoon entrance."

Now that the action was over, Sally felt weak. For the first time she noticed the delicious whiffs of meat and vegetables simmering over the campfire. Her stomach ached with emptiness. "I'm starving," she said.

"Me, too," said Andy. "What's to eat?"

"*Freebooter* stew," said Peter. "The best there is."

"Oh boy," exclaimed Andy, "oh boy! Three cheers for Chef Peter!"

While they ate, Peter told them his news. "When you were away I saw the Geminis settling into the camp around the corner," he said. "I guess they won't have so far to come when we move out."

"*If* we move out," said Sally.

Peter put his spoon down very carefully in his bowl and looked at her. "If?"

"Yes, if. We'll have to talk to them about it. No matter what we promised, we can't leave while we still have a sick dolphin to look after. And she's going to have a baby as well."

Peter gave a long, low whistle of surprise. "Heck," he said, "they're not going to like this."

"Is it war?" asked Andy excitedly. "Is it war?" He tugged at Sally's shirt. "Are we going to fight them?"

"Andy! That's enough!" She'd had about all she could take of Andy for one day. "It's your bedtime." But even as she said it she yawned deeply. She knew she'd be following right behind him.

She awoke soon after dawn, before the sun had climbed above the battlements of white trade-wind clouds that fringed the horizon. The light was still gray and the warm air hung heavy with the slow-drifting fragrance of waxy frangipani blossoms growing on the other side of the island. She sniffed deeply and let the thick, sweet taste slide down the back of her throat and fill her chest.

A curl of smoke lifted gently from the white ashes smoldering in the fireplace. Peter had banked dirt on the ashes to keep them glowing all night, but the fire had licked through in one place.

She walked past the fire, down to the cool sand of the beach and then to the right, where Daniel was.

But Daniel was no longer there. The dolphin's long black shape was missing. A wave of panic swept through Sally and she started to run toward the hollow in the sand.

Then, out of the corner of her eye, she caught a jerky movement in the water on her left. She stopped short. It looked like a big fish just under the surface.

No, not a fish. A dolphin! A baby dolphin! And there, cruising in slow circles just a little farther out, was Daniel.

Sally waded excitedly into the water and the baby darted away, but Daniel swam into the shallow water to meet her and let Sally stroke her. She looked better, but still very weak.

"Well done!" cried Sally. "Oh you clever, clever dolphin!"

She sprinted back to the tent to wake the others. "Quick," she said. "Come and see Daniel's baby."

Andy jumped up as if a snake had bitten him and took off running. Peter staggered after him slowly, rubbing his eyes.

As they watched, the little dolphin darted in little circles close to Daniel. Then he came in close and nuzzled her flank.

"Hey, he's biting her!" cried Andy, hopping with indignation. "Hey, cut that out!"

Sally laughed. "No, silly," she said, "he's just practicing feeding. He's learning where to find his breakfast."

"Daniel needs some breakfast, too," said Peter, yawning loudly. "I'd better find my fishing pole."

"And I'd better fetch some netting from *Freebooter*," said Sally. "We don't want these two escaping. Andy, you come and help me."

The netting was like fishing net. It came in flat lengths and Dad lashed it to *Freebooter*'s lifelines to keep the sails from falling overboard when they were pulled down.

Sally found a piece of the right length that they could string like a tennis net across the entrance to the lagoon. She also found some spare lead weights like the ones Peter used for fishing. They could tie those on the bottom of the net to make it hang down straight.

They locked *Freebooter*'s sliding hatch and jumped back into *Redwing* for the sail to the lagoon. Mr. Whitely, the hotel manager, waved to them as they passed the hotel jetty, and Sally said, "Good morning," very politely.

At the entrance to the lagoon, Sally strung the net on a long piece of rope.

"Now we need some loops in each end," she said.

"I can do it," said Andy, grabbing the rope. "I'll do you a bowline knot. I know how."

"I'll do it for you," said Sally.

"No, I want to do it myself. I know how. I do, truly."

"Just give it here." There was no knowing what crazy kind of knot Andy might do.

She placed the loops over heads of coral on either side and threw the net in the water. It hung nicely, blocking off the entrance completely, with the top just out of sight below the water level.

They finished in good time. The tide was coming in and starting to creep up over the reef. In another hour they would have had to work underwater.

"There," she said happily. "A good job well done, as Dad would say."

Andy pouted. She looked at him and shook her head in irritation. He was being difficult again. It was so childish. Just because he hadn't been allowed to make the knots.

They pulled *Redwing* up on the beach in awkward silence. Andy stalked off to the tent. Sally fetched a bucket and went off to find Peter.

She found him on a patch of dark brown rocks where the reef joined the beach. He was leaning back contentedly against a sunny rock, with his floppy white hat pulled down over his face. His fishing line was out on the seaward side of the reef, in the deep water that fell steeply from the side of the reef.

She walked right up to him without being noticed, lifted his hat, and asked, "Any luck with Daniel's breakfast?"

"Oh, hi!" He stretched lazily and reeled in his line to see if there was any bait left. "Not this time," he said. He slipped a plump piece of mussel meat on the hook. "But I caught plenty earlier on."

"Where are they?"

"Well, *some* of them are over there in that rock pool."

"And the rest?"

"Inside a stupid pelican's belly. That one, over there."

On the far side of the rocks a brown pelican the size of a turkey was watching Sally cautiously. He had a large, comical face with a huge beak and a pouch slung below it that made him look lopsided.

"He watched me put the fish in the pool, and then he went and helped himself," said Peter. "He's a real sneaky fish thief. When I saw what was happening I put a branch of a palm tree over the pool."

Sally stood up to inspect the pool and the pelican took off. Perhaps he did look awkward on land, but he could certainly fly beautifully. He glided gracefully down the length of the beach at the water's edge, as if he were on patrol. His wings were long and wide and he hardly ever seemed to have to flap them. He started to scan the shallows close to the beach for shoals of fish. Without warning, he crumpled in midair and fell into the water with a huge splash in an untidy muddle of feathers, beak, and feet.

Sally was so taken by surprise that she burst out laughing. "Did you see that?" she cried.

"Sure. That's how he does his fishing. Just falls with his beak open."

Sally slapped her thigh. "Why doesn't he break his neck? That water's only a couple of inches deep."

Peter shrugged. "Beats me. But he does it all the time. I think he's a loony."

Sometimes, after a dive, the pelican would float upside down for a moment, with his head under water and his big webbed feet waggling helplessly in the air. Then he would right himself and float facing into the wind. He'd look very thoughtful and slightly foolish while he strained the seawater from his bulging pouch and swallowed his meal of fish.

The pelican's constant companion in all this was a sea gull, a scruffy-looking laughing gull with a dark head and only one foot.

He was small, as sea gulls go, but Sally could see that he'd lived a hard life. When the pelican was doing his beautiful swooping glides along the beach, the gull would fly behind in a series of ragged, hoppity lurches to the left and right.

He cawed and cackled all the time, urging the

pelican to catch more fish. But the big bird took no notice of him; not even when, to Sally's amazement, he perched excitedly on the floating pelican's head, hoping to grab a few fishy morsels as they fell into the sea.

Sally lifted the palm branch and put four fish in the bucket for Daniel.

"That pelican of yours must think he's died and gone to heaven," she said. "He's finally got a boy of his own to catch fish for him."

"Shoo!" said Peter, waving her away good-naturedly. "You're a fine one to talk. Go feed your whale."

When Sally arrived with the fish, Andy was crouching in the shallow water of the lagoon, watching Daniel with her new baby. The two were swimming in a large circle near the shore.

Andy had gotten over his fit of the sulks. Luckily, they never lasted long with him.

"Are the dolphins doing okay?" asked Sally.

"Yes, they're fine," said Andy. "But the name's not."

"The name?"

"Daniel. Daniel's not a good name for a mother dolphin."

"Have you thought of anything else?"

"I thought of Danielle. You know, with two *l*'s and an *e*."

"And so?"

"Well, Peter said it was too fancy-sounding for a dolphin."

"I think Daniel is just fine," said Sally. "I think we should leave it. It's unlucky to change the name of a boat. Or a sea creature," she added hastily. "It's like starting a voyage on a Friday. If you do, it's real bad luck."

Andy looked relieved. "Good," he said. "Then I have a name for the baby, too. Daniel Junior." He looked at her hopefully.

"I like it," she said. "We'll call him DJ for short."

Daniel swam into the shallow water as soon as she saw what Sally was carrying. She caught the first fish as Sally threw it. She bit each one just once and then gulped it right down.

"She must have been starving," said Sally.

"So am I," said Andy. "Isn't it time for lunch?"

"I'll make you a sandwich. Go and call Peter."

It was just after lunch, when Andy was lying on the grass beside the tent, with his book of knots in one hand and a ginger beer in the other, that he heard the engine.

Sally watched him sit up and listen carefully.

"Recognize it?" she asked.

The noise was getting louder, coming in from the open sea.

"It's a boat. I've heard it before," said Andy. "But I can't think when." Andy was one of those people who can remember the sounds different engines make. "It's a big motor," he added. "Going fast."

"Look," said Sally, "Daniel can hear it, too."

It worried the dolphin. She was excited, swimming in small circles and nudging DJ toward the gap in the reef.

"Hey, now I remember!" said Andy.

And as he said it, Sally saw a motorboat racing toward them at top speed. It was on a collision course with the reef, which was just barely covered by the incoming tide.

6

WHITE LIGHTNING'S DISASTER

"It's the same boat!" yelled Andy. "It's the one that ran over Daniel!"

"What's he doing?" Sally watched with growing alarm. The speeding boat cut the corner of the island, not knowing that just in front was an invisible reef covered by a couple of inches of water.

She was coming toward them fast, planing in a cloud of white spray. Sally could see a man and a woman in the front seats. The woman wore a scarf over her head. It fluttered wildly in the wind.

Sally jumped up and waved her arms to warn them away. Andy shouted: "Watch out!" But the scream of the high-powered motor drowned his voice.

The speedboat smashed into the underwater

reef at thirty knots and ripped her bottom open with a grinding roar.

In slow motion, Sally saw two things she'd never forget. One was a body flying through the air and landing in the lagoon with a huge splash. The other was Daniel leaping over the net and disappearing out to sea.

There was a blinding flash as the boat's fuel tank exploded. It made a deafening *whump!* and shook the air so solidly that Sally felt it bang against her chest.

Black smoke poured from the cockpit. Burning oil and gasoline spread over the surface of the water to leeward. Chunks of wood and fiberglass rained down and splashed into the lagoon, making overlapping circular ripples.

Then there was a deep and eerie silence.

After a moment or two Sally could hear a groaning noise coming from the wreckage of the boat. Then, dimly, she heard Peter shouting as he ran along the beach from Black Rocks.

Sally felt dazed. For several seconds she stood paralyzed. Then she ran to the lagoon, bounding into the water with giant steps. As the water deepened she waded furiously toward the body.

It was a man, floating face up. He was wearing an orange flotation vest. He was unconscious, but breathing. She grabbed his wrist and pulled.

When she reached the shallows she handed him over to Andy. "Pull him up on the beach," she panted. "Get his head out of the water."

She turned back to swim to the reef. Peter arrived, breathing hard, and pulled off his shirt. He plunged after her.

She didn't have a plan or any time to think of one. She just knew she had to reach the burning boat. When her canvas sneakers brushed the coral she stood up and picked her way carefully to the boat.

Flames and smoke shot out of the bows and hissed as the shallow water lapped at them. The whole stern of the boat had been torn out. The motor and transom lay upside down yards behind. The damaged aluminum propeller stuck up awkwardly in the air, spinning slowly like a toy windmill on a stick.

At the front end of the cockpit, the woman with the scarf lay slumped forward in her seat. Her eyes were closed. She was bleeding from a cut on her forehead.

Peter yelled, "Let's get her out of there! The flames are getting close!"

Sally shook her head. "She's too heavy. I don't think we can lift her over the side."

"Maybe we can slide her between the seats and out the back."

But when they looked, a jagged head of coral was sticking up through the cockpit floor at the back.

Sally jumped in and tugged at the woman's legs. "Help me," she said. Peter grabbed her arms. They dragged her back into the cockpit, a little farther away from the fire. They tried to lift her over the side of the boat, and managed to raise her a little, but then her limp body flopped back.

"We're not strong enough," said Sally despairingly.

"Let's try to put out the fire," said Peter.

They climbed out onto the reef and made their way to the bows, where flames were licking the painted name: *White Lightning*. With their cupped hands they splashed water on the fire.

The acrid smell of burning fiberglass made Sally cough. Her lungs burned and her eyes watered. But the heat of the fire just made the water sizzle and turn into steam. Sally scooped water on her face to cool it.

Then, suddenly, Andy was standing beside her, saying, "Aren't you going to get her out?"

"C'mon," she said. "All three of us together. We can do it."

With Sally lifting the woman in the middle, and Peter and Andy at each end, they lifted and slid and rolled her, higgledy-piggledy, up the side of the cockpit and across the narrow deck.

Her legs splashed into the water. Sally tugged at the woman's shirt. The rest of her body followed. She floated facedown in her life vest in the shallow water. Sally quickly spun her over onto her back and listened to her breathing. She undid the woman's scarf and retied it over the wound on her forehead.

They towed her away from the burning boat. When they reached the deep water of the lagoon they floated her out, hung on to her, and kicked their way slowly toward the beach.

When, at last, they pulled the woman up on the sand alongside the man, Sally's legs felt like jelly. She sat down quickly in the warm water and held her head in her hands.

She looked up to see Peter standing in front of her.

"Want me to go to the hotel for help?"

"Yes, thanks. As fast as you can."

"I'll be quick." He raced off to the path that led around the western edge of the island.

Andy stood beside her and flipped water with his foot. "Are they all right?"

"I think so—for the moment," said Sally. "The woman has stopped bleeding and the man looks okay. But they need a doctor."

"It's them," said Andy. "The ones I saw from Lookout Point. The ones who ran over Daniel and didn't bother to help. I wrote the name in the log. *White Lightning*."

"They tried to take a shortcut across the reef," said Sally. She shook her head in disbelief.

"Serves them right," said Andy.

"Now, now! They could have been killed."

"So could Daniel," said Andy unrepentantly.

Sally still felt a little dazed. So much had happened so quickly. There were several vivid scenes crowding her mind. One came back to her now. It was of Andy appearing beside her on the reef.

"Hey!" she cried. "How did you get across the lagoon to the reef? You can't swim!"

Andy was taken aback for a moment. "I don't know," he said. "Didn't think about it. When I saw you over there I just came." He grinned happily. "I guess I must have swum."

"Dog paddle?"

"I don't know. Just *did* it," he said proudly.

The motorboat from the hotel arrived with Peter and two men aboard. Peter slipped over the side and dropped the net so they could bring the boat in to the beach.

The men loaded the limp bodies of the man and the woman on the boat and set off at top speed for the Mission Harbor hospital. Sally swam out to help Peter replace the net. And only then did she remember the other thing that was bothering her.

"Daniel's gone," she said flatly.

"Gone?"

"Yes, escaped."

"When?"

"Just as the boat crashed."

"Oh, no!" Peter smashed the water savagely with his fist. Spray shot high in the air. "Oh, no!" he groaned again.

In her mind's eye, Sally could see the dolphin curving gracefully in a powerful leap over the net. There hadn't been time to think about it then, with so much happening.

But now a desperate sadness crowded in on her. Her throat felt swollen and her lips began to tremble. She couldn't keep them still. She stroked them hurriedly with her fingers and pressed them together in a tight line.

"Let's see if DJ's okay," said Peter. His voice was shaky.

They swam to the beach together in silence, doing a slow breaststroke.

Andy joined them as they walked along the beach to Daniel's hollow. He hopped along in front of Peter. "I can swim," he announced proudly.

"Oh yeah? You said you could do a Turk's head, too."

"Well, I can."

"I thought they were very hard to do," said Sally.

"Not if you know how."

He felt in his pocket and pulled out a length of cod line. He began to wind the line around his finger, holding the short end down with his thumb. He wound it around three times, crossing it over itself and tucking it under several strands. Then he pulled it off his finger, stared at it, straightened it out, and started again. "Blue blistering bilge water!" he shouted. "It won't go right."

"Are you sure you can do one?" said Sally.

"I did one last night."

"Hmm," said Sally.

"I did, I really did."

"Hmm," said Peter.

"And I can swim, too. Ask Sally."

Peter looked at her. "Have you *seen* him swim?" he asked.

"No, but he got over to the reef, remember?"

"Heck! So he did. I didn't think about that."

"Neither did I," said Andy. "I just did it. It was easy."

"Can you do it again?" asked Peter.

"Of course."

They had to sit down and wait while Andy showed them. At first he floundered a little, holding his breath and dog-paddling along parallel with the beach in chest-deep water. He couldn't swim and breathe at the same time. Then he got the hang of it again and started breathing as well as swimming.

Peter stood up and clapped. "I guess you get to go solo in *Redwing* now," he said.

Sally wished he hadn't said that. It was true that Dad had promised Andy he could sail *Redwing* on his own when he'd learned to swim. But she wasn't sure Andy could be trusted yet. Swimming was one thing. Sailing a dinghy was quite another.

And *Redwing* was a very special dinghy. She'd been given to Dad by his own father thirty years earlier. She was a classic design, made of overlapping wooden planks and copper nails. She was *Freebooter*'s tender now. She worked hard at ferrying people and gear between the yacht and the shore.

People from other yachts would often stop and run their fingers over her varnished mahogany topsides. Then they would stand back and stare, the way farmers lean on a gate to watch a prize bull. They'd look very wise and shake their heads and say: "They certainly don't build 'em like that anymore."

If anything happened to *Redwing* while Dad was away, Sally didn't want to be the one to take the blame.

Andy came to shore, grinning and shaking his hair like a wet Labrador. He held a skinny arm aloft in a gesture of triumph.

"See—I told you," he said. "I definitely can swim."

"Yup," said Peter. "Pretty definitely. That's great."

Andy looked very pleased with himself.

All three of them walked along the beach, looking at the wreckage of the *White Lightning* out there on the reef.

The fire in the bow had almost burned itself out now. A pall of thick black smoke still hung over the reef, though, and a thin smear of rainbow-colored gasoline drifted out to sea.

They found DJ darting about anxiously in the deeper water, looking for his mother.

"We'll have to let him go," said Sally. "We should have left the net down."

Peter scratched his head and looked out to sea. "What if he can't find her out there? He can't feed himself yet. And she could be miles away already."

"Still running away from the engine that ran over her," said Andy.

"Yes, she recognized it," Sally agreed. "Maybe she thought it was coming back to hurt her again."

"We can't let DJ out to die," said Peter.

They all thought about it for a bit.

"You may be right," said Sally. "But what else can we do? He'll definitely die of starvation in here."

7

~~~~~~

A FOSTER MOTHER FOR DJ

Sally sat down at the edge of the lagoon and pulled her bare foot across the ridges in the sand. She watched the lean black shape of the little dolphin darting back and forth underwater. He was making the same sort of ear-piercing squeaks Daniel had made the first time they saw her, only higher in pitch.

"He's talking to us," said Peter. "I bet he's asking for food."

"He'll be all right for a while," said Sally. "Dr. Watkins told me that newborn mammals can last twenty-four hours before they need to be fed."

"Can't we catch some fish for him?" asked Andy.

"He can't eat fish yet," Sally answered. "He's too small. He needs his mother. He needs milk."

Peter scratched a shoulder blade thoughtfully. After a while he said: "We've got milk."

For a moment, Sally didn't know what he was talking about.

"Powdered milk," he continued. "There's plenty on *Freebooter*."

"Feed him, you mean? From a bottle?" That might work. If they could feed him until he was big enough to catch fish for himself, then they could let him go out to sea on his own to find his mother.

"Only trouble is, we don't have a baby bottle," said Sally.

Peter rubbed his hands slowly on his pants. "Perhaps we could get Daniel to come back in," he said. "Maybe we could throw some fish in the sea near the gap in the reef."

"Like bait, you mean?"

"Sure, that should attract her."

Not much hope, really, thought Sally. She shaded her eyes with her hand and squinted against the sun at the miles of sparkling sea outside the lagoon.

Daniel could catch all the fish she wanted out there. And she'd probably be with her family already. Dolphins always travel in families and hunt fish together. Peter was thinking like a fisherman.

And dolphins aren't fish. No matter what Nurse Jenkins thought.

Peter looked at her carefully. "You don't like that idea?"

"Well . . ." She shrugged.

"Okay, here's another one. How about a recording?"

"Of what?"

"Of DJ. You know those little squeaks he makes? She'd hear those all right. Sounds travel a long way underwater. She'd know it was her baby looking for her."

There was a small tape recorder on *Freebooter.* Dad used it for recording radio weather forecasts. They could borrow that.

"We could play it back in a plastic bag underwater," said Peter enthusiastically.

"And drop the net to let her in when she comes to see what's happening," added Sally.

"Can I help with the recording?" asked Andy. "Can I? Can I? I can swim out and record DJ."

"Hold your horses!" said Sally. "First we must think of a way to *feed* DJ."

"And me," said Andy, rubbing his stomach. "I'm starving, too."

"All of us," said Peter.

He was right. It was nearly suppertime. The sun

was glowing red and starting to dip down behind the high black mountains of Tortuga. The trade wind was slowing down in preparation for a good night's rest. The palm trees were straightening up after bending over and trying to touch their toes all day.

Peter's pelican and his sea gull friend were making their last sweeps along the beach, flying with the sun behind them to surprise the fish. Sally watched with interest. Peter had named them Percy and Sam.

Andy ran ahead to light the campfire. Sally and Peter followed more slowly.

"A ginger beer bottle," said Peter suddenly. "Why couldn't we use a ginger beer bottle?"

"To feed DJ?"

"Yes."

"Because we haven't got a nipple for the end."

"I thought of that first," said Peter. "We can use the thumb from one of Dad's rubber gloves."

"Hey, all *right*! We can prick a hole in it with a needle," said Sally.

She felt happier now that they had a plan. But could you really bottle-feed a dolphin like a lamb or a calf? She'd soon find out. First thing in the morning, she'd fetch the powdered milk from *Freebooter*.

*   *   *

Redwing's thwarts were still damp with dew when Sally raised sail. Glistening beads of cool moisture fell from the folds of the mainsail and pattered down on her head and arms.

The red-brown sail glowed with the fire of the rising sun and dried quickly. The little jib rustled in the gentle breeze as the trade wind sleepily roused itself for the day's work.

Sally sniffed and breathed deeply. She loved the fresh new smell of the morning. On Crab Island there was always a spicy-sweet scent of frangipani; and soon that fragrance would be mixed with the clean tang of wood smoke from the breakfast fire.

She stepped lightly into the boat and hauled in the sails. *Redwing* gathered way quietly. Tiny wavelets smacked noisily against the underside of her lapstrake planking. *Redwing* was chuckling to herself.

Sally headed for the gap and raised the centerboard and the rudder for a moment as they slipped over the net. *Redwing* made long, lazy tacks against the breeze, past the reef sticking out from Elbow Point, and around to the eastern side of the island, where *Freebooter* was lying quietly at her mooring opposite the little hotel.

Just a few yards from the yacht, Sally luffed *Redwing* up into the wind and nestled her gently alongside the two plastic fenders that hung from the lifelines.

It pleased her when she did that well. Sometimes a gust of wind would come at the last moment and she came in too fast and smacked hard against the side of the yacht. But this morning it was perfect.

Sally climbed aboard *Freebooter* and watched happily as the wind blew *Redwing* back to the end of her painter. She slid back the heavy hatch and went down below. She found Dad's recorder and a heavy waterproof bag that usually contained the walkie-talkie radio. The recorder fit inside beautifully.

The large container of powdered milk was in its place in the cool, airy locker under the bridge deck. Sally filled a half dozen plastic bags to take back with her.

All this she put in a knapsack, along with two rubber gloves and a book Peter had asked for. Then, as an afterthought, she added two bottles of ginger beer from the ship's stores.

The run home was quick and easy. Peter had cooked some oatmeal porridge for breakfast. Sally's was waiting in the pot, keeping warm at the side of the fire.

It was the wonderful kind of oatmeal you get only when you're camping. Sally let it run over her tongue slowly and slide down her throat. It was sweet and creamy and tasted faintly of wood smoke. She had two helpings, with lots of sugar.

Making a feeding bottle for DJ was fairly easy. She sterilized a ginger beer bottle by boiling it in water for ten minutes. Then she sliced the thumb off a rubber glove and pricked a hole in the end with a needle. Peter mixed the milk powder with fresh water. He wanted to add a teaspoon of sugar. "For instant energy," he said.

But Sally wouldn't let him. "Dolphins don't eat sugar," she pointed out.

He filled the bottle three-quarters full and fastened on the nipple with thin whipping twine from *Redwing*'s sail repair bag.

DJ was swimming quietly a few yards out from the beach.

"I'll fetch him," said Andy. "I can swim *and* breathe now."

"You're doing very well," said Sally. "I'll teach you the breaststroke."

"I want to do the crawl."

"Breaststroke first. It'll keep you afloat longer in rough water. Dad said so."

Andy pulled a face and tried an experimental crawl anyway. After two seconds of thrashing his arms and legs, he came up spluttering and spitting out water.

"Breaststroke first!" Sally repeated. She stared at him and sighed loudly. What was it about Andy that you had to tell him everything three times?

Andy went back to the only stroke he knew. He dog-paddled out around the little dolphin and herded him into the shallows, where Peter and Sally guided him to Daniel's old hollow in the sand. He wasn't afraid of people. He has no reason to be yet, Sally thought.

She shoved the bottle of milk underwater and waved it in front of DJ. He showed no interest. Then she squeezed some milk into the water in front of his face and all at once he understood.

He fastened on to the nipple and tugged. He swam away, then zipped back in a tight circle. Once again he sucked and tugged but wouldn't settle down.

"Something's wrong," said Peter, bending over with his nose almost touching the water.

"Not enough milk getting through the nipple," said Sally. At least, that was what she hoped it was. They could cure that.

Peter held the needle with a pair of pliers from the tent tool kit and heated it in the fire. He poked it through the nipple again several times, making four holes in all. Then he made each of the holes larger.

This time it worked. DJ homed straight in on the bottle and sucked it dry within a couple of minutes.

"Wow!" said Peter. "That was fast."

"He must have been starving," said Sally.

For the next hour they did nothing but refill the bottle and feed DJ.

"How long is this going to go on?" asked Peter. He had volunteered to be DJ's foster mother. That meant sitting around patiently in shallow water, holding bottle after bottle, while DJ snuggled between his outstretched legs and suckled.

Sally tried to think. She knew a human baby weighing eight pounds needed one bottle every four hours. "How much do you think he weighs?" she asked.

Peter rubbed the top of his head to help himself think. "About forty pounds," he said eventually. "Leastwise, a fish of that size would weigh about forty pounds."

"Peter! He's not a fish!"

"I know. I was just comparing."

Sally screwed her eyes up in concentration. "Well, then he needs *five* bottles every four hours."

"Wow! We need to get Daniel back here quickly," said Peter. "I don't want to be stuck here feeding a baby dolphin forever. I need time to fish."

They spent the rest of that morning making

extra feeding bottles. In the end they had ten. Andy offered to drink more ginger beer so they'd have more bottles, but Sally said ten was quite enough, thank you. In any case, they had run out of fingers and thumbs from the rubber gloves.

It was Peter who found out that DJ didn't need him as a foster mother after all. DJ could feed himself if you could make the bottle float nipple-down. Peter made it do that by getting some strips of metal from his fishing box and wrapping them around the neck of the bottle.

"That's great," said Sally. "Now we can float out enough bottles to keep him going for twelve hours."

But Peter wasn't satisfied with his first dolphin-feeder, the Mark 1 as he called it. He told Sally he was working on an improved model, the Mark 2. It had a new invention to stop the bottle floating all over the lagoon.

"I'm going to patent it. It keeps the bottle in one place and it's very kind to the environment," he explained. "It won't pollute anything, it's guaranteed rustproof, and it never needs its batteries changed."

"Sounds interesting," said Sally seriously. "What is it? What stops the bottle floating away?"

"It's a piece of string tied to a stone!" cried Peter. He laughed outright and slapped his leg. "Caught you!"

"Didn't."

"Did, too."

"This is very childish," said Sally, getting up briskly. "Come on Andy, help me find nine more stones."

They walked together down the beach toward Black Rocks, where Percy Pelican liked to perch and dry out in the sun. There were stones and big pebbles down there in the rock pools.

"I have an idea for making the feeding bottles better, too," Andy announced.

"Oh yes?" said Sally warily.

"I'm going to tie a Turk's head on every bottle," he said.

"What for?"

"They're magic," he said simply. "DJ needs a whole lot of magic to bring his mother back."

They were on their way back with the stones when the Geminis' catamaran appeared around the corner of the island. Sally got such a fright she dropped her stones.

"Oh no, I forgot!" she cried. "We promised to get out of the camp by today."

The fast-moving catamaran slid stealthily along the outside edge of the reef. The twins sat side by side and headed for the gap in the reef. But when they saw *Redwing* on the beach, and the tent still in place, and Sally and the boys in the lagoon, they turned away.

"Wave and shout!" said Sally. "Tell them to come in. We need to talk to them. We need to explain about Daniel and DJ."

But no matter how they yelled and waved their arms, the Gemini twins refused to take any notice. They turned their boat around and sped back the way they'd come, toward their camp around the corner of the island.

"They deliberately pretended not to see us or hear us," said Peter indignantly.

"Yes," said Sally. She gazed at the disappearing catamaran. "I'm afraid that means trouble."

8

ANDY GOES SOLO

It was pleasantly cool in the checkered shade of the palm trees at the campsite. The sun was high and hot, but here on the grass next to the tent the wind came sifting through the trees and blew cool drafts on Sally's bare arms.

She was helping Peter with the after-lunch washing up. She was rinsing the plates and placing them on the grass to dry. At least, that's what she was *supposed* to be doing.

In fact, though, Sally was staring out over the lagoon. Her eyes were fixed on nothing in particular. Sally was thinking. And when Sally had to think really hard, everything else just seemed to stop.

She became aware that Peter was standing in

front of her. His head was tilted over to one side and he was scratching it.

"You all right?" he asked. "Want me to finish for you?"

"Oh, no, I'm okay, thanks." She grabbed a plate, rinsed it, and put it down next to the others.

It was Andy she was thinking about. He had taught himself to swim and now he kept asking her if he could go for a sail in *Redwing*. On his own.

Going solo under sail was a big thing in the Grant family. It was like a religious ceremony or a coming-of-age. People treated you differently after you'd gone solo under sail.

But Dad was away and Sally was in charge. People sometimes said she was impulsive. And she admitted it was true. But she was never impulsive when she was looking after her brothers.

The trouble was, she didn't know if she could trust Andy. What if he capsized? Who would rescue him? What if he ran on the coral and sank Dad's precious dinghy?

"What are you dreaming about?" It was Peter in front of her again.

"Andy. Do you think it would be all right if he went solo under motor only?"

"Why not under sail?"

"I don't think he's ready."

"He'd be fine. He can sail."

Sally knew it was true. But she'd rather wait until Dad got back.

"I think he'd *like* to use the motor," she said.

"It's not the same thing. You know that."

That was true, too. Dad always said they were sailors, not stinkpotters.

But her mind was made up now. And when Sally's mind was made up, she was ready for action, right or wrong.

She yelled for Andy and he came hoppity-skipping up from the beach, dragging a piece of driftwood for the fire.

"We need more powdered milk for DJ," she said. "Will you fetch some from *Freebooter*?"

She tried to make it sound casual, as if it were something that happened every day. "It'll be quicker if you take *Redwing* and motor around," she added.

Andy stopped dead in his tracks. "Er . . . take *Redwing*? On my own?"

"Yes please. And do hurry."

The driftwood fell right out of his hands. He grabbed the key Sally held out. It would open *Freebooter*'s main hatch.

"Can I sail?" he asked quickly.

"No, the motor will be faster. Just use the motor."

"But—"

"Andy!"

He hesitated only an instant. Then he flew down to the boat without even asking how much milk powder she wanted. Sand sprayed in all directions with every footstep he took.

Sally and Peter pottered around the camp pretending to be very busy. But they watched him like hawks.

He seemed to remember all the rules. He put the life jacket on first. He checked that the oars were on board. Then Sally saw him unscrew the cap on the gas tank and stick his finger in to see if there was enough.

It was high tide and he got *Redwing* afloat with one little push. He stowed the anchor carefully and coiled the line beside it in the bows.

He glanced up to see if they were watching him and Sally turned quickly away.

"Ha!" said Peter. "He's lost a fender. Look, it's floating in the lagoon."

But Andy had seen it. He grabbed it and threw it aboard.

"That's funny," said Sally. "I didn't know there was a fender on *Redwing*."

Then there was the rasp of the engine starting, followed by the metallic *tinkety-tinkety-tink* of its idling. Andy checked to see if the cooling water was spurting out properly.

He put the motor in gear, opened the throttle, and headed for the gap in the reef. Sally held her breath. Would he remember the net? Would the propeller get hooked on it and leave *Redwing* drifting helplessly toward the reef?

He cut the motor a few yards before he reached the gap, tilted it clear of the net while *Redwing* crossed over, and started it again on the other side.

"That was neat," said Peter admiringly. "Good job he didn't forget the net."

Sally laughed nervously.

They walked to the tent together. Peter took the tape recorder and the plastic bag and walked down to the lagoon. Sally took the binoculars and hurried to the pathway that led to the hotel.

Redwing was motoring nicely, trailing a faint haze of blue exhaust smoke. White foam curled upward and outward from the bow. It spread parallel tracks of white lace in *Redwing*'s wake.

Sally saw Andy standing at the tiller, bouncing slightly on the balls of his toes. He was the odd one out in the family. He loved motors. He'd told her often before that his favorite scent was the smell of gasoline mixed with sweet new motor oil.

He kept rubbing his nose casually, she noticed. With the finger he'd dipped in the gas tank. Probably to get a better whiff.

He waggled the tiller experimentally and the bow swung back and forth. He looked ahead, saw a pelican resting on the water, and steered a wide arc around it.

He disappeared out of sight around Elbow Point, carefully staying clear of the off-lying reef. Sally sighed. He certainly seemed to know what he was doing. But she'd feel better when he and the dinghy were safely back.

Down in the lagoon, Peter was holding the recorder underwater in its plastic bag and patiently trying to make the baby dolphin squeak.

"Perhaps he's making noises that we can't hear," said Sally. "Dolphins can make noises too high for the human ear."

"Well, that's no good," said Peter. "We won't know we've recorded anything unless we can play it back and hear it. In any case, he does make plenty of noises we *can* hear."

"Only when he wants to. You can't make him."

DJ darted into deeper water as a black shadow raced toward him. Percy Pelican was swooping down to see what was happening. Sam Sea Gull was fluttering along frantically in his wake.

Peter waved his arms to shoo Percy away. "He's making DJ nervous," he complained.

"Percy probably thinks you're getting too

friendly with some big black fish," said Sally. "He's jealous. Don't let him find out you're actually *feeding* DJ or you'll be in big trouble."

Peter thought about that for a moment. "Hey, that's an idea!" he said. "How about fetching a bottle of milk for DJ? That'll make him squeak."

It did, too. When Sally plunged it underwater for a moment and then pulled it out again, DJ squeaked loudly in protest.

It was a noise that's hard to describe.

"It's like a cricket chirping," said Sally.

"It's like a squeaky axle," said Peter.

In truth, it was like a mixture of both.

Peter recorded it and then they let DJ have his bottle.

The recording session was interrupted when *Redwing* appeared off the reef again.

Andy brought her in perfectly. He was trying to look casual, but his lips kept peeling back of their own accord and parting in a wide grin.

"How did it go?" asked Peter.

"No problem," said Andy.

"I saw you drop the fender in the drink," said Peter, nudging him.

"I didn't, either," said Andy indignantly. "It was just floating in the lagoon. I rescued it."

Sally said, "Where is it now?"

"I put it with the others on *Freebooter*, in the cockpit locker."

"Good. And congratulations on your solo."

"It wasn't a proper solo," he pointed out. "Not under sail."

"Time enough for that," said Sally gruffly. "Right now we have some important recording to finish."

At four o'clock, when it was DJ's proper feed time, they recorded some more squeaks. Each time they offered him a new bottle, DJ wriggled and squeaked with anticipation.

Peter stood up slowly and straightened his back. "I wish we knew what these noises meant," he said. "I hope he's not saying: 'These kids are teasing me and not giving me my food when I want it.' "

"No, that wouldn't help to get his mother back," said Sally. "But I don't think it matters what he says. She just needs to hear his voice, that's all."

"I hope you're right."

"Dr. Watkins said scientists believe each dolphin family has its own language. So Daniel should recognize him when she hears him."

"I hope Dr. Watkins is right, too."

"Anyway, we've got a recording at last," said Sally. "Now we have to think of the best place to play it back—so Daniel will hear it."

"Somewhere near the gap in the reef," Peter suggested. "That's where we want her to come to."

"I guess you're right," said Sally. "We'll start tomorrow morning."

Andy had finished fussing with *Redwing* and was carrying a large can of powdered milk up to the camp. "I brought the whole can," he explained. "You didn't say how much you wanted."

"That's fine. DJ's eating like a horse."

Andy collected more wood for the fire and lit it in preparation for supper. When the first dry twigs were flaming and sparking nicely, he settled down to make some more Turk's heads on DJ's feeding bottles.

"How's the magic coming on?" said Sally.

"I can do them without the book now," said Andy proudly. He showed her a finished knot on a bottleneck.

There were three lots of three strands, cleverly running over and under each other in an ancient pattern.

"Look," he said, "you can't see where it begins or ends. That's the magic."

"Let's hope it works," said Sally.

After supper, when he ran out of bottles to put Turk's heads on, Andy looked around for something else. Sally pointed to Peter's fishing pole, propped up against the side of the tent. That could always use a bit of magic, too.

She lay awake for a long time after they'd all gone to bed that night, wondering where Daniel was now. It would be awful if she were trying to get into the lagoon to find her baby and the net was in the way. Or would she just jump over it, as she had done when *White Lightning* crashed?

Someone spoke quietly, as if in reply to the question in her mind, but she couldn't make out what the voice said. Sally blinked her eyes and looked around. Peter and Andy were sound asleep.

There was the voice again. But it wasn't in the tent. It came from the reef. And there was another one. Was she dreaming?

She lay very still in the pitch blackness, wondering whether she should wake her brothers. The canvas walls of the tent suddenly felt very thin.

Then she heard them again. She shivered. No doubt about it. There were voices coming from the reef.

9

MYSTERIOUS VISITORS

Sally lay rigid in her sleeping bag, straining her ears to hear the voices above the background rumble of the surf breaking against the reef.

Could it be the Gemini twins coming to raid the camp? Her heart began to pound heavily in her chest and she caught her breath.

She was wondering whether she should jump up and look out of the tent when Andy stirred. He sat up, rubbing his eyes, and saw Sally lying propped up on one elbow.

"What are you doing?" he whispered.

"Listening," said Sally softly. "I heard voices outside."

"So did I. Who is it?"

"Can't tell."

Then the low sounds of conversation traveled crisply through the night air again.

"One of them's a woman," said Andy.

"Yes. Maybe it's the people we rescued from the powerboat. Let's take a look."

They crept outside the tent, leaving Peter fast asleep, rolled in a tight ball in his bag.

Sally focused the binoculars on the reef. They were *Freebooter*'s night glasses. They were at their best in the dark.

A low tide had exposed the light-colored reef. Sally could see two people—really just vague, dark blobs—near the wreck of the boat. A man and a woman, she thought.

"What are they doing?" asked Andy.

"Searching the wreck of *White Lightning*, I think. Lifting things. Looking for something."

"Why did they come at this time of night?"

"I don't know."

A rubber dinghy was grazing the seaward edge of the reef. Somewhere in the background there was another, fainter noise, a hint of low rumbling.

"Can you hear the engine?" asked Sally.

"Yep. Two motors. Just idling. They're spitting out exhaust water. You can hear it."

"Is it one boat, or two?"

"One boat with two engines, I think. Can you see it?"

"No. It's too black out there."

"Can I have a look, can I, can I?"

"Yes, yes! Here." She handed over the glasses. "But don't drop them," she warned.

Andy scanned the horizon behind the reef, where the boat should have been. But it was too dark. "I can't see it," he admitted reluctantly. "But I'm sure it's there."

There was no knowing how long the people had been on the reef. But after she and Andy had been watching for about ten minutes the voices stopped and the rubber dinghy silently disappeared seaward.

They sat there talking softly for a while, too excited to go straight back to bed.

"I'm glad it wasn't the Geminis," said Andy.

"Me, too." There was no knowing what the Geminis might have done.

After a while they went inside and crept back into their sleeping bags, wondering what the mysterious visitors had been looking for, and whether they'd found it.

Andy fell asleep right away, but Sally lay awake for ages, listening very carefully and staring at the dim starlight twinkling through the ventilation hole above her head.

If they really were the people they'd rescued from the wreck, why were they creeping around in the middle of the night? And why hadn't they come to say thank you?

She decided that from now on, she and her brothers would have to take turns standing night watches again: two hours on watch and four hours off. The Geminis were bad enough. But if grown-up people were going to be raiding their reef at night, she needed to know about it. She drifted off into a restless sleep.

After breakfast next morning, Sally and Peter carried DJ's feeding bottles down to the lagoon. DJ had gotten pretty good at emptying floating bottles.

Peter sat in the shallows with the first one and let DJ nestle in his lap. He stroked him while he fed. Within minutes, though, Percy swooped down for a splashy, feet-first landing. He floated in front of Peter and stared him in the face accusingly.

Every now and then Percy wagged his huge beak slowly from side to side. "What are you doing, you strange bird?" asked Peter.

"He's saying he doesn't like what *you're* doing," said Sally. "He's saying if you can feed some dumb fish, you can feed him, too."

"Well, maybe he's right," said Peter. "Maybe a little fishing wouldn't do any harm. . . ."

He floated the rest of DJ's bottles into deeper water, where the little dolphin could feed himself in peace, and walked back to the camp to get his fishing pole.

Percy waddled up the beach behind him with love in his eye and hope in his belly.

Sally and Andy rowed *Redwing* out to the gap in the reef and anchored over a patch of sand in knee-deep water on the northern side.

Sally carried the tape recorder, in its waterproof plastic bag, to the edge of the reef, where the coral fell away suddenly into the deep, crystal-clear water of the sea.

She pressed the button to play back DJ's voice. Then she lowered the recorder about fifteen feet into the sea on a length of thin rope. When it got caught on coral heads and sea anemones she jiggled it patiently until it fell past.

Andy poked at things with the toes of his sneakers.

"Be careful," said Sally. "Some of that coral's sharp. It could infect you." She'd warned him about that a dozen times at least. And every time he'd pulled faces at her.

While the recorder played, they watched the waves for signs of dolphins. Sometimes, when a pod of dolphins was hunting, twenty or thirty of them would leap and crash and frolic in the waves, swimming around in a circle with a shoal of fish in the middle. They gradually tightened the circle, making it smaller and smaller, to herd the fish tightly into one spot. That made it much easier to catch them.

But today there was no sign of dolphins. There was nothing jumping in the waves, no quick blasts of air from blowholes.

Sally pulled up the recorder, rewound the tape to the beginning, and lowered it again. Still no luck.

After the third try, they gave up. "Let's go," said Sally. "We're wasting our time."

"Good," said Andy. "This is boring."

Sally rowed them back, glad of the chance to stretch her arms. She rowed well, keeping the oar blades low over the water.

Andy suddenly yelled: "Freebooters! I nearly forgot to tell you. Freebooters. That's what we should call ourselves. You know—like the Geminis."

"It's all right if you like bloodthirsty pirates," said Sally. "But I think we should have a different kind of name, not one that comes from our yacht. Something more original."

"That's what Peter thinks, too," said Andy gloomily. "It's hard to think of a name."

They dragged *Redwing* up above the high-water mark and wandered down the beach to see if Peter was having any luck at Black Rocks.

"Hey!" he shouted when he saw them coming. "Somebody put a Turk's head on my pole."

"Guess who!" yelled Sally.

Andy dashed on ahead of her. "Did it bring you any luck, did it, did it?"

"Sure did," said Peter. "Look in the rock pool."

Sally lifted the palm branch and peered in. Six good-sized fish were swimming there.

"And Percy's had his breakfast already," Peter added.

"He doesn't think it was enough, though," said Sally. The big bird was floating in deep water at the edge of the rocks, just where Peter would pull the next fish out.

"Yes, he's greedy," Peter complained. "He keeps trying to snatch the fish I catch before I can get them off the hook." He waved his arms and shouted: "Shoo!"

Percy reluctantly paddled away a few feet, looking hurt and surprised. Then he just slid back quietly to the same place again. He settled his wings on his back with a few quick shakes and gazed shortsightedly at Peter.

"You're a dimwit, you know that?" Peter shouted. "You're a big nuisance." But he said it with fondness in his voice.

Percy swung his head from side to side, studying him with one beady eye at a time, looking very serious.

Peter put down the pole and threw his hands in the air helplessly. "Okay, I give up," he said to Percy. "I guess it's time for your after-breakfast snack."

He stepped over to the rock pool and threw three wriggling fish into the air, one by one. Percy caught them expertly, stowed them in his pouch with an air of great concentration, and flew off to a quiet corner of the lagoon, with Sam in close and anxious attendance.

Peter sliced two of the remaining fish into bait-sized pieces and put them in a bucket.

For the next half hour Sally and Andy threw handfuls of bait into the sea near the gap in the reef, hoping to attract Daniel.

But the sea seemed dead that day. The wind wasn't blowing as strongly as usual, Sally noticed. There were fewer birds around, too. It was like the calm before the storm.

"Well," she said finally, "if Daniel *is* out there she's not giving herself away."

"Maybe she's not hungry," said Andy, hurling the last bit of bait far out to sea.

And maybe she's not even alive, thought Sally.

Sally had just filled DJ's bottles with milk and was tying the teats on them, when Peter and Andy came running up from the beach.

"Visitors," said Peter curtly. His face was serious.

"And they've been here before," said Andy.

Sally heard once again the low throb of idling diesel engines. A trawler-type motor yacht of about forty feet was stealing up to the reef from the east.

Her black hull crouched low in the water. Sparks of sunlight flashed off the corners of her varnished wheelhouse. The name *Black Thunder* stood out in bold white letters on her bow.

She felt her way in confidently, stopping fifty yards short of the reef. Two people launched a black rubber dinghy from her cockpit.

One jumped in and started to row quickly through the gap in the reef.

10

~~~~~~

GLORIA PAYS A VISIT

Sally stayed close to her brothers in front of the tent while the dinghy came closer. When it was half-way across the lagoon they could see there was a woman in it.

"It's her—the woman we rescued," said Sally quietly.

They walked down to the water's edge together to meet her. She was a blond with lightly tanned skin. Her cheekbones were high and her hair was scraped back from her face into a bun. She had a large adhesive bandage on her forehead.

Sally remembered how she'd looked the day before yesterday, after *White Lightning* hit the reef. Her face was covered in blood then, and her hair was matted in thick strands over her cheeks.

Now she looked beautiful, but quite severe. There was something about her face that warned you not to joke with her. She looked like a science teacher Sally once had known.

Sally knew instinctively that Mom wouldn't have liked this woman.

Nevertheless, the woman came toward them with a smile. It was a tight-lipped kind of smile, but a smile nonetheless.

"Hello," she said, "I'm Gloria. I've come to thank you. . . ."

"Hi," said Sally, "are you all right now?"

"Yes, I'm fine. And Benito, also. That's my friend. He's on the boat. He says thanks, too."

"Did they keep you in the hospital?" asked Andy.

"Just overnight. We weren't burned. Just shock and concussion. We were very lucky."

"It's a pity about the boat," said Sally. "There wasn't anything we could do."

"Yes," said Gloria, "but we still have the other one." She pointed at *Black Thunder*.

"We have another one, too," said Andy. "A forty-five-footer. She's moored in front of the hotel."

"Oh, really?"

Gloria *sounded* like that science teacher, too. The

way she said "Oh, really?" left you confused. You couldn't tell whether she was terribly bored or terribly interested.

She walked toward the camp, brushing sand from her white shorts with irritated little swipes.

"You look, um, very comfortable here," she said. "Do you all sleep here? On your own?"

"Just us," said Andy proudly. "We don't have a mother and our father is away. We look after ourselves."

"Oh, really?"

Sally could see that Andy was enjoying the attention he was getting from this woman.

"Would you like some ginger beer?" he asked, as she peered inside the tent.

"I'll share a bottle with you," she said. And then, to Sally's astonishment, Gloria reached into the tent for a sleeping bag. She spread it on the grass and sat down on it.

Sally had to check her first impulse to rush over and jerk the bag out from underneath her. How dare she just reach in and grab a bag without asking?

But just then Peter caught her eye and made an anxious face. She could tell what was bothering him. He, too, had the uneasy feeling that Andy was giving away too much information.

He was spilling the beans to this rude stranger who said she had come to thank them, but who hadn't stopped asking personal questions.

Sally tried to talk to Andy when he fetched the ginger beer but Gloria was watching. She wanted to remind him that this was one of the people who had nearly killed Daniel. This woman's attention had gone to his head. How could he forget?

It was time to feed DJ, but Sally didn't want to leave Andy alone with Gloria.

"By the way, did any of you find a fender?" Gloria asked offhandedly.

"Yes, I did," said Andy brightly.

"How very clever of you," said Gloria, flashing him a warm smile. "Do tell me all about it."

Andy grinned with pleasure. "Is it yours?" He paused for a moment and then said: "Heck! I forgot. I put it aboard *Freebooter*. I didn't know whose it was. If you want, I'll—"

"*Freebooter?*"

"Our yacht," said Andy. "She's a Bermudan cutter."

"Oh, really?"

Sally ground her teeth. Gloria had said it again. It was time to interrupt.

"There were people on the reef last night," she said. "Was it you?"

Gloria seemed to be caught off-guard. But she

recovered quickly. "No," she said. "Certainly not."

Peter joined the attack. "Was it you who ran over the dolphin? In *White Lightning*, I mean."

Gloria pulled her lips into a thin line. "A dolphin? I don't know anything about a dolphin."

"She was pregnant," said Sally. "She nearly died. And the people who hit her didn't stop to help her."

Gloria stood up. "I really must go now."

She's lying, thought Sally. We know she's lying about hitting Daniel. She's hiding something. Which was just what you might expect from a woman with snow white shorts, red lipstick, and matching nail polish.

No decent, honest person ever managed to keep her shorts that clean while living on a boat. Never mind the nail polish.

Andy stood up with her. "I can do Turk's heads," he announced.

But Gloria had lost interest. She turned away without replying.

They walked down to the beach and watched her row back to *Black Thunder* with large, amateurish swoops of the oars.

"Hey—she forgot to ask me to get the fender from *Freebooter*," said Andy.

"Maybe she's not really interested in getting her old fender back," Peter suggested.

"Oh, I thought she sounded *very* interested in getting it back," said Sally.

"Maybe it's full of golden doubloons." Andy's eyes widened. "They've dug up some pirate booty. They've hidden it in fenders."

"Can't be gold, silly," Peter pointed out. "That's too heavy. It would sink."

"Well, never mind that now," said Sally. "C'mon, you two, DJ's starving."

They fetched the bottles from the camp and ran back to the lagoon.

"Watch this," said Peter. He bent over and splashed the top of the water several times with his hand held out flat. DJ heard him and came sprinting into the shallows. "He's learned the food signal. He'll come from anywhere in the lagoon."

He sat down in the water and helped DJ feed from the first bottle. Sally knelt alongside him and stroked the baby dolphin slowly. He felt just like Daniel, cool and tough and slippery, like a black, blow-up boat. Only he was more wriggly than Daniel.

"I hope we find your mama soon, you poor thing," she said softly. She knew how tough it was to lose a mother.

*   *   *

Chef Peter was planning to serve fish stew that night. "The recipe book says it's much better with parsley," said Peter, "but we don't have any."

"There's some dried parsley on *Freebooter*," said Sally. "I'll fetch it."

"Good," said Peter. "And some salt, too, while you're there."

"We should make our own salt," suggested Andy, who was passing by with a dead branch in tow. "Like they do on Salt Island. Just let the sun dry up pools of seawater."

"I figure we don't have time for that," said Peter. "Forget Salt Island. If you don't hurry up with that firewood there won't be any supper tonight here on Crab Island."

Sally was glad of the excuse to go to *Freebooter* alone. She peered into the cockpit locker and found the fender Andy had thrown in.

It was just like one of *Freebooter*'s fenders, a thick, white, plastic sausage. It had a rope spliced to one end. It was a bit blackened in one or two places— scorched by the fire, maybe—but otherwise it looked quite normal.

It was a bit heavy though. Not heavy enough to be filled with gold but heavier than usual. *Freebooter*'s fenders were blown up with air. They were much lighter.

At first she thought some water might have leaked in; but when she shook it there was no noise of sloshing. Perhaps it was packed tight with cotton like some old-fashioned life preservers were.

She was tempted to slit it open to see if anything strange was inside. But if she did, there was no way to repair it. Gloria might complain to Dad. That was just the sort of thing she *would* do.

So Sally took it back to camp just as it was. She'd clean it up first thing tomorrow and have it ready for Gloria's next visit. She stuffed it in *Redwing*'s bow locker and sailed home.

"Three cheers for the parsley barge!" shouted Andy as *Redwing* tacked into the lagoon.

"Catch the bow, noisy landlubber!" Sally cried. "How dare you call this fine ship a barge? Here, gallop to the ship's cook with this rare bottle of precious herbs."

"Did you remember the salt?" asked Andy.

"Sure did."

"Shall I take it now? Or do you want me to do two gallops?"

"Please yourself."

"Okay, I'll do two," said Andy, whipping his imaginary horse into action. "First the parsley gallop."

*   *   *

That night, after a delicious supper of stew with fish caught and cooked by Peter, they started keeping watch again. Sally stood the first watch, from eight to ten. She sat near the tent, where the grass bank joined the sand of the beach.

The warm trade wind was gently rustling the dry branches of the palm trees around the camp. Now and then the breeze bore faint rushing sounds of surf breaking on the reef far away on the hotel side of the island. On this side of the island the water over the reef was calm and black. Little wafts of wind ruffled Sally's hair where it hung out of her woolen cap. It tickled her neck.

The air smelled like newly washed sheets. There was a faint whiff of something clean, sweet, and perfumed, some tropical night flower Sally couldn't identify.

Over the sea, the night was very dark. Pinpricks of light twinkled far away to the southwest, on the island of Tortuga. High up on the mountains, away from everything else, a lonely line of red lights flashed on and off to warn aircraft to keep clear.

Every quarter hour or so Sally picked up the night glasses and scanned the lagoon and the horizon. She could vaguely make out the feathery form of Percy perching on the black rocks at the western end of the beach. *Redwing* lay quietly, half out of the water. Her bows made a dark V against the sand.

When the rubber dinghy spurted through the gap in the reef, Sally was taken completely by surprise. Two people were rowing, sitting side by side. They sped along stealthily, making no noise.

In the background, just a darker patch on a dark ocean, was the distinctive shape of *Black Thunder*. She was stopped, with her engines switched off and lights out. Anchored, thought Sally. And behind her was a lighter patch. Another yacht?

Cold sweat broke out on her brow. Her stomach cramped tightly as if she were going to throw up. It was hard to breathe. She watched, frozen to the spot, as the dinghy hit the beach.

Two people jumped out. They moved swiftly and very quietly toward the camp. One of them held something shiny. A gun.

Sally leaped to her feet and ran.

11

KIDNAPPED!

Sally ran wildly, blindly, tripping and stumbling in the dark. She didn't know where she was going, except that it was away from the people with the gun. She didn't think about her brothers or *Redwing* or anything. She just fled. The blood pounded in her ears. She ran along the track to Lookout Point.

Her foot caught in a deep crab hole and she fell hard. For a while she lay there, face down in the middle of the sandy path, fighting back sobs.

Then she remembered her brothers. She had panicked. She had deserted them. The sobs rolled out now and she didn't care if anyone heard. She pulled herself to the side of the path and cried loudly.

But gradually, as the sobbing subsided, she began to feel a different kind of fear. It was no longer fear for herself, but fear for her brothers. And soon that fear turned into anger.

She sniffed loudly and defiantly, not caring if anyone could hear. And very deliberately she started back to the camp.

But her steps slowed as she got nearer. She could hear voices: Gloria's voice, high and raspy, and a man's voice lower and speaking more slowly.

Sally stopped behind a palm tree at the edge of the clearing. They were all in the tent. Someone held a flashlight that made big shadows on the walls. In the still night she could hear them clearly.

"It's on *Freebooter*, it is, it is! I put it there."

"It's not. You're lying! We searched it." That was Gloria.

"What we shall do now?" The man. Benito. He had a foreign accent.

"Take them with us," said Gloria.

"To Scorpion?"

"Yes."

"And their yacht, too?"

"Yes, yes. For goodness' sake stop asking questions and listen. The girl must know where the fender is. But she's run away."

"What if she calls the police?"

"Just listen, will you? She won't. Not yet, anyhow. Not until she knows where her brothers are.

We'll leave her a note. Warn her not to call the cops, or her brothers will suffer. Tell her we'll be back tomorrow at noon. If she gives us the fender, she'll get the yacht and her brothers back."

Sally's blood ran cold with fright. She shivered and her stomach contracted in spasms. She tried to think, but her head was whirling. She could remember that Andy had put the fender on *Freebooter*. He *wasn't* lying. But there was something else, something more about the fender, something that wouldn't come to mind. It was important. If she could just concentrate . . .

Her head spun with dizziness, and the acid taste of sickness came to her mouth. The world started turning cartwheels around her. Her knees buckled, and she slid down suddenly with her back to the tree.

When she opened her eyes again, they'd gone. All of them. She got up very slowly and walked to the edge of the beach, recovering her strength.

She looked through the night glasses. *Black Thunder* and *Freebooter* were no more than fuzzy blobs against the black sea. *Freebooter*'s mast blanked out the stars one by one as it swayed from side to side.

She knew her brothers were there. She could

see wings slowly beating against the stars just behind *Freebooter*. Percy Pelican was faithfully following his new friend Peter.

Out of the corner of her eye she saw *Redwing* stir slightly on the beach. The tide was coming in. And then she remembered.

She remembered that she'd put the fender in *Redwing*.

She clutched her chest and sighed a great gasp of relief, then she ran through the sand with giant steps and thrust her arm into *Redwing*'s forward locker. Yes, yes, the fender was still there.

But now she felt confused. Half of her, the impulsive half, wanted to race after the kidnappers and rescue her brothers. The other half, the more cautious, motherly half, thought it might be better to call the police, or wait until they all came back tomorrow.

But she couldn't call the police. She had panicked and deserted her brothers. *She* had to make up for that somehow.

And another thing—she could surprise Gloria and Benito. They wouldn't be expecting her if she came after them. They thought they were safely hidden. But she knew where they were. Ha!

As usual, Sally's impulsive half won the battle. The feeling of helplessness passed. Now she felt much better. Her head was clear again. She knew exactly what she had to do.

She had to go to Scorpion Island to rescue her brothers.

She had to get there quickly, while it was still dark.

She'd take *Redwing*.

The note was on the front of the tent. It was in Peter's handwriting. It said:

Don't call the cops or anything silly. We have your brothers and the boat. We will exchange them for the fender. Be here alone at noon tomorrow.

She stuffed it in her pocket and went to work. First she had to take care of DJ. She made ten bottles of milk and floated them in the lagoon for the baby dolphin to find in the morning.

She made two sandwiches for herself and filled a gallon plastic jug with water. These she stowed aboard *Redwing*. When the boat was ready to go, she went back to the tent for one last time to fetch a sweater and a waterproof jacket.

While she was zipping open her bag at the back of the tent, the walls fell in on her. Canvas collapsed all around her, blacking out the flashlight. She dropped the light and scrambled for the doorway, fighting to breathe. But the folds of canvas trapped her.

In the background were loud voices, but she was too busy to identify them. She was trying to force a way through the clinging material before she suffocated.

"Tell them to get out, tell them to stop fighting!" The voice sounded familiar.

Sally pushed and shoved frantically with her hands and legs in the pitch blackness. She felt strong, as if she could rip the fabric apart with her hands. But when she tried, she couldn't. And her way out was blocked.

And then another voice was saying: "One at a time, you hear? Come out one at a time!"

Someone held open the doorway and she burst through, dragging fresh air deep down into her lungs.

"Whoa!"

"Stop there!"

At last she recognized the voices. It was the Gemini twins.

"Don't do anything," she said, "it's me."

"We know who you are," said Jon. "And you're still in our camping place."

"Lie down on your face," said Jan. "We want to tie your hands."

"Tell the others to be coming out now," said Jon. "Slowly, like. One at a time."

"There's nobody else here," Sally gasped. "Just me. My brothers have been kidnapped."

There was a long silence.

"Let me up," said Sally.

"Kidnapped?" said Jan.

Jon was patting the fallen tent. "Nobody else in there?" he said, half to himself. "You made all that commotion by yourself?"

"I've got to rescue them," said Sally desperately.

Jan got off Sally's back. "It's funny," she said. "We came to raid *you*. To make you move out of our camp."

"We couldn't move earlier," said Sally. "We waved at you and tried to tell you, but you wouldn't look."

Jon sat down beside her. "So you've been raided already? Tell us the story," he said. "Slowly, like, so we can understand."

Sally explained about the dolphins and the fender and Gloria. And she added, "Now I must hurry. I must get to Scorpion before it's light."

"But it's getting on for twenty miles to Scorpion," said Jon. "You can't go on your own."

"I've sailed to Mission Harbor alone before."

"Yes, but that's in sheltered water, like. Scorpion is over the open sea."

"It's a long way," said Jan. "You can't go alone."

"I can."

"No you can't, it's too dangerous."

"I can do it."

"I'll come with you then," said Jon.

"Me, too!" cried Jan. "I'm coming, too!"

"We'll take *Gemini*," said Jon. "It's high tide. We can sail her out."

"Yeah," added Jan, "she's much faster than your old boat and she's not half as tippy."

Things were going much too fast for Sally's liking. She didn't know if she could trust the twins and their boat. Only a few minutes ago they had been enemies. Now, suddenly, they were her friends.

But she didn't have time to brood over it. "C'mon," said Jon, walking through the palm trees in the direction of the Gemini camp. "We better get going."

"Wait!" cried Sally. She ran to *Redwing* and came back with the water, the food, and the precious fender.

"D'you know the way to Scorpion in the dark?" asked Jan.

"Oh sure!" said Sally brightly. She wanted to get

going. She didn't want anything to stop them now. But she didn't feel as confident as she sounded.

"Good," said Jon. "You can be the navigator."

Sally had seen Scorpion Island on *Freebooter*'s big chart of the islands. It was about three miles long and a mile wide, so they could hardly miss it. It had a spit of land that curled around its back, like a scorpion's sting.

The cruising guidebook said the island was deserted. Fishermen stayed there from time to time, but nobody lived there permanently.

The trouble was that it was very low lying and dangerous for yachts to approach. The first thing you saw from the sea was the tops of palm trees. But that was only in daylight, of course. Sally figured they wouldn't be seeing any trees at night.

Jagged coral reefs lay all around the island. There were only a few passes through the reefs. Hundreds of ships had been wrecked on Scorpion in the days when pirates fought with Spanish treasure ships around here.

In a small boat it was safer to get near the reefs, though. Small sailing dinghies could turn quickly and get out of danger. Dinghies were shallower and easier to manage than a large yacht or a pirate brigantine.

So her plan was simple: As soon as they found the outlying reef, they would run alongside it until they found a pass. Then they'd go into the lagoon and land on the beach.

Sally watched the twins get *Gemini* ready. They put on the rudders and raised the sail without having to speak a word. They obviously knew their jobs.

Jon handed her a life jacket. "Here," he said, "put it on. We always carry a spare."

It felt very strange to sail on a catamaran. The Hobie 14 had a deck made of canvas strung between the two hulls. It was springy, like a trampoline. You sit *on* a catamaran, not *in* it, as you do in an ordinary dinghy like *Redwing*.

They rushed out over the dark reef and the two hulls hissed with speed. They left twin grooves of phosphorescent lights twinkling and tumbling in their wake.

The big mainsail hummed with power from the steady trade wind and Jon released the sheet only when a puff started to lift the hull they were sitting over. It was an unusual feeling not to heel over when the puffs came. On *Gemini*, the puffs of wind just turned into power and made her spurt forward.

The night was pitch black. Spray rattled onto the deck when a wave hit the bow. Rushing along at this speed is like driving blindfolded down the freeway, thought Sally.

"You sure we're headed in the right direction?" asked Jon. "I see nothing ahead, just plain nothing."

"Just keep the wind abeam," she said. "Just keep it on the side. Trust me. We'll be fine." She crossed her fingers firmly.

"Okay, navigator, I trust you."

Gemini plunged on recklessly into the darkness of the ocean.

12

~~~~~~

SHIPWRECK!

They had no compass or any other way to tell where Scorpion was. But Sally knew the trade wind always blew more or less from the same direction. And the course to Scorpion lay at right angles to the trade wind.

They were all used to judging where the wind was coming from, day or night. Sally could tell by the way her hair tickled her shoulders or neck. So they could steer the right way, even if they couldn't see anything.

"But how will we know we're near the reef?" asked Jan. "If we run onto it full tilt we'll be wrecked."

"And nobody to rescue us, like," added Jon.

Sally knew some simple navigation. Dad had taught her. And the simplest of all was called dead reckoning. That was what Christopher Columbus had used on his way to these islands.

"If we know the speed of the boat, and we know how long we've been going, we can easily work out how far we've come," Sally explained.

"Well, we know how fast *Gemini* goes," said Jon. "We've often timed her. Right now we're doing eight or nine knots."

Jan pulled out her watch and peered at the luminous dial. "And we've been sailing for two hours."

"Then we've come between sixteen and eighteen miles," said Sally. "Better say eighteen."

"Only two miles to go then?" said Jon. "I still can't see anything. It's as black as the inside of a cow out here."

"You won't see anything until the last minute," Sally warned him. "Even in daylight you'd only see the tops of the trees."

"We'd better reduce speed for the last bit, then," said Jon.

Sally thought about it. She wanted to get there as fast as possible. But she didn't want to hit the reef at full speed.

"Give it another ten minutes like this," she said, "then we can slow down."

Gemini's wake hissed loudly as thousands of tiny air bubbles tumbled and turned and fought each other to get to the surface. The catamaran rose and fell regularly on long swells coming from the same side as the wind. The mast and rigging made a deep thrumming noise. A tiny soprano jingle of vibration came from the tiller bar.

Sally tried to concentrate on the navigation. She didn't really want to think about the mess she was in. Dad was due to come back in two days.

To what? No *Freebooter*. No Peter. No Andy. No Daniel, even. What would he think of her? Would he ever trust her again?

What would Mom think if she were still alive? It didn't bear thinking about.

It was nearly 12:45 when they slowed down. Jon let the powerful sail out until it was almost hanging straight away from the wind.

Gemini stood on toward the invisible reef in pitch darkness at slow walking speed. Jon waggled the rudders to keep her going straight. *Gemini* didn't steer easily at slow speeds.

Sally strained her ears for the noise of surf breaking on the reef. Only their ears would tell them when they were close.

But she couldn't help staring into the blackness as well. Once or twice she thought she saw lights on shore, but she didn't tell the others.

She knew the lights came from looking too hard.

Dad had told her about that. You always saw a light on a dark night at sea if you stared too hard.

The test was to look a little off to one side. Then, if the light was still there, it was real. It was the same for the stars, when you were trying to find a faint one at dawn or dusk. If you looked to the side you'd see it quicker.

But now, when Sally looked to one side, there was nothing.

The mainsail fluttered slightly and *Gemini* almost came to a standstill. Jon tugged at the tiller and slowly she turned away from the wind. The sail filled and went back to its quiet work. Yard by yard, they crept over the sea toward the reef.

What would happen if they hit it? If *Gemini* were lifted on a swell and smashed down on the reef, her fiberglass hull would be in splinters in minutes, Sally thought.

But surely, if you were moving slowly you'd be able to hear the waves breaking on the reef and turn away in time to avoid hitting it? Wouldn't you?

"You sure we're near the island?" Jon's voice was low and strained. "We could be anywhere. Lost at sea, like."

"We can't miss," said Sally, trying to sound confident. If her sums were right they *must* be near Scorpion. You had to trust the sums. No matter how hopeless everything seemed, you had to have trust. What else was there to do?

The minutes dragged as if they were all sitting blindfolded in dentists' chairs. A dollop of spray hit Sally on the side of her face. It dribbled down the back of her jacket and made her shiver.

Jan whispered to Jon, "Do you suppose we could find Crab Island again if we wanted to? Or Tortuga?"

Sally knew why she was asking. She was scared. They were all scared. *Gemini* should have arrived at the reef by now; and there was no sign of anything.

She felt her breath coming a little quicker and her throat tightening. Now her ears were beginning to play tricks from listening too hard. She thought she heard the sea breaking in front of her, to the right. Then the same noise, a bit fainter, came from the left. To the right again. To the left.

It didn't make sense. She pressed her hands against her ears.

She listened again. Yes, there *was* something.

"Hey, look out!" yelled Jon.

Jan screamed loudly.

Straight ahead the waves were crashing on coral. "Turn away!" yelled Sally. "Turn away!"

"I'm trying to!" Jon had the tiller hard over. But

Gemini was dragging her twin hulls around too slowly.

She hit the coral a glancing blow, bounced off, and drove forward again.

Now there was deep water—then more surf breaking in front of them. "Turn! Turn!" yelled Sally.

They'd found a gap in the reef. That's why she'd heard surf on the left and the right.

But the gap was a narrow one, too narrow for the slow-turning catamaran. Her bows crashed into the coral reef in front of her. She stopped dead in her tracks. Sally catapulted forward and tumbled heavily against Jan.

Jan looked back and cried, "Jon! Where's Jon?" There was no sign of him.

Gemini's starboard stern, slammed by wind and waves, crunched onto the reef behind. She was jammed sideways in the gap.

A swell lifted her and dropped her on the reefs. Loud splintering and grinding noises erupted from both ends. The coral punched jagged holes in her hulls. She began to sink. A loud, hollow clang rang out as the aluminum mast toppled onto the reef.

Jon appeared in the water alongside the boat. "Swim in through the gap!" he spluttered.

"Keep together!" Sally shouted. "Keep together!"

She and Jan jumped overboard in their life jackets and swam in through the gap. All three of them clung in a tight circle on the lagoon side. They watched as *Gemini* slowly settled lower in the water. It seemed to take ages.

"Oh, wait! Wait!" Sally remembered the fender was still tied to the catamaran's deck. She *had* to get the fender.

She swam back clumsily in the jacket. She felt in her shorts pocket for her sailing knife and slashed the rope holding the fender.

"Come back!" yelled Jon. "She's sinking!"

"Coming!"

Sally kicked her way back to where the twins were floating in the calm waters of the lagoon.

"Is everyone okay?" she asked, hugging the fender.

"I'm fine," said Jon.

Jan didn't say anything but she nodded her head.

They swam in slowly to the beach, a lighter strip in the blackness, and threw themselves down.

Dry, powdery sand stuck to Sally's wet hands and face in little cakes. They lay in the sand for a long time, catching their breath and not saying anything.

Sally could see the reef now, where the water was white and boiling luminously. And there was the dark, smooth patch, the passage through the reef that *Gemini* had found on her own. But now there was no *Gemini*.

Redwing would have brought us in here safely, she thought. *Redwing* would have turned quickly. She'd done it before, when they'd brought Daniel back from the hospital. The catamaran was clumsy. It just couldn't turn fast enough to keep clear of the reef.

But she didn't say any of this to the twins. They were sitting huddled close together—dark, bulky, miserable lumps in their life jackets, not speaking. She could imagine how they felt about losing their boat. What would their parents say?

Sally moved closer to them, still clutching the fender.

"I'm sorry," she began.

"Not your fault," said Jon gruffly. "There just wasn't time. . . ." His voice trailed away.

"What now?" asked Jan. "What do we do now?"

"First we must find my brothers," said Sally. "That's why we came."

"Nothing else we *can* do," said Jon.

They set off to explore.

Coconut palms separated the beach from the dense bush that covered the middle of the island.

The only way to get anywhere was to walk along the beach.

Sally had no idea where they had landed on the island. But she had a feeling they were near the eastern end. That's where she had aimed for. So she decided to go west, keeping the wind behind her and on her right.

At the water's edge the sand was fine and firm and they made good progress. They walked in single file with Sally leading the way. After about a mile, after they'd been walking for twenty minutes or so, the noise of the surf on their left died down and Sally knew they had come to another gap in the reef.

The beach bore away to the right, however, skirting a large, sandy bay. They followed it around. Underfoot they felt shells through their sneakers in some places and little round pebbles in others.

Sally listened hard for any sound above the noise of the sea surging against the reef behind them and the wind rustling in the tops of the palms. All her senses were alert. She sniffed deeply and her throat tasted the salty, musty, seaweedy tang of the rock pools out on the reef.

A faint light was glinting erratically out in the bay on their left. A navigation buoy, perhaps. No, it was too faint. Perhaps she was looking too hard again.

She looked to one side of it and in the corner of her eye she could see it flicker again. Now she looked straight at it. It was the light of a star reflected in a mirror. No—glass.

The glass was swaying gently, suspended in midair. Sally drew a deep breath. It was the windshield on the wheelhouse of a large motor yacht at anchor a hundred yards off the beach.

Sally dropped onto the sand and pressed against it very hard. She could feel her heart thumping against the cold sand. Jon and Jan dropped down alongside her.

Sally pointed and whispered: "*Black Thunder*! They may be watching out."

Jon nudged her. "What's that?"

Sally looked where he was pointing. It was a lighter patch, fifty yards away from the motor cruiser. *Freebooter*!

"Let's get off the beach," said Sally quietly. She was afraid anybody watching from the boats could spot them against the light sand.

They moved cautiously to where the dark trunks of the coconut palms joined the beach. They lay there, watching in silence.

Sally rested her chin on the fender. She could see *Freebooter* better now. She was lying to her own anchor and pointing in toward the beach. But where were the boys?

There was no building on the beach, nor any clearing in the bush behind it. Her brothers had to be on one of the boats. But which one? And were they guarded?

There was an unfamiliar shape on top of *Freebooter*'s cabin. Sally stared at it for several moments. Could it be a man, sitting down? It was impossible to tell in the darkness at that distance.

But as she watched, the shape stood up, flapped its wings busily, and settled down again.

"Hey!" said Sally with excitement in her voice. "It's Percy! Good old Percy!"

"Who's Percy?" said Jon.

"A pelican," Sally explained. "Peter's pelican. Now I know where Peter is."

She hoped Andy was with him.

13

~~~~~~

PREPARING TO ESCAPE

Sally didn't have to think about what to do now. "Let's go," she whispered urgently.

The three of them waded silently into the warm, calm water. They were still wearing their life jackets. Sally pushed the fender in front of herself as she swam toward *Freebooter*.

Percy spotted them coming and flapped off quietly into the night, landing in the lagoon with a faint splash. When they reached *Freebooter*, Sally put her ear to the yacht's hull.

There were no sounds of anyone moving on board, only the usual faint cracking noises from pistol shrimps. While the twins floated in the water, ready to swim away into the dark night at a moment's notice, Sally climbed the ladder on *Freebooter*'s stern.

She stood dripping in the cockpit for a moment. She quietly set down the fender in a corner of the cockpit. Then she looked over the sliding hatch. It wasn't locked. She slid it back three inches and peered inside. Behind her the way was clear to dive overboard if she had to. She peered inside again. Nothing but blackness.

She slid the hatch back with her thumbs an inch at a time, until there was just enough room to squeeze through.

She crouched on top of the companionway steps, holding her breath. A small pool of water collected at her feet. It started to drip steadily onto the step below. It was a quick, steady rhythm, drumming into the silence.

There was nobody in the quarter-berth, nobody in the saloon. She crept forward, feeling awkward in the life jacket but not wanting to take it off yet.

Damp footprints trailed her as she stole past the galley and the navigator's desk, past the big teak table, past the toilet and shower compartment.

She found Peter and Andy on the V-berth up in the front of the boat, unable to move, gagged and trussed like a couple of turkeys ready for the Thanksgiving oven.

Their eyes were opened wide.

"Are you alone?" Sally whispered anxiously.

They nodded vigorously.

"Wait—I'm coming back."

She retraced her steps to the cockpit, leaned over the side, and called the twins on board. They all took off their life jackets and left them to drain on the cockpit floor.

Sally loosened her brothers' hands and their gags. Then she left them to untie their own legs while she went back on deck to check on *Black Thunder*, anchored just fifty yards to the right. All was quiet over there.

Sally felt much braver in the warm cabin she knew so well. She opened a can of corned beef and cut it into chunks that they all ate with their fingers. It disappeared in a few minutes. She opened another. She showed the twins how to work the galley pump and they all had long drinks of fresh water.

"They pointed a gun at us," Andy said excitedly. "They tied our hands behind our backs and marched us off like prisoners and—"

"How did you get here?" interrupted Peter, rubbing the stiffness out of his wrists.

"We sailed—on *Gemini*."

"Wow!"

"Where's the fender they wanted?" It was Peter again. "We told them the fender was on *Freebooter*.

But they searched her and couldn't find it. So they just took the whole yacht."

"Wait, wait, we'll talk about all this later," said Sally. "First we've got to escape." She was thinking hard. "How many are there on *Black Thunder*?"

"Just the two. You know them. Gloria and Benito."

"Are we going to sail away? Are we, are we?" That was Andy piping up, struggling to speak with a mouth filled with corned beef.

"Yes, but first we've got to strand them here," said Sally. "If we just sail away they'll come after us and catch us. They've got a motorboat. It's twice as fast as *Freebooter*."

"Whoa," said Jon. "Back up a bit, like. Strand them here?"

"Yes, we've got to. Otherwise they'll just come after us and bring us back."

"We've never sailed *Freebooter* on our own before," said Andy.

"We can do it. We know how." Sally paused for a moment. "Um—can you remember how to start the engine? All the sea cocks that have to be opened and things?"

"Yes, I know, I remember. I'll show you."

"No, not yet! Listen to me, Andy. For goodness' sake don't do anything until you're told."

There was a quiet rustle of feathers and a gentle splash in the water alongside the yacht.

"Percy thinks we can do it," said Peter. "He thinks it's time to go home."

"We can't, yet," Sally was thinking hard. "C'mon everybody. How can we stop *Black Thunder* from following us?"

They sat down around the big teak table in the main cabin and whispered in the darkness.

"Tie her to the shore," said Andy. "To a palm tree. I know a knot—"

"They'd just cut the rope," said Sally. "Be serious."

"Sink her," said Peter. "Swim over with a drill and bore a hole in the bottom."

"Too slow. They'd notice. They've got pumps. And they might hear."

"Bomb her with exploding ginger beer bottles."

"Andy!"

"Put a chain around her propellers," said Jon.

Nobody said anything for several moments. Each could imagine the grinding, tearing damage a tough steel chain would do to soft bronze propellers. Even hitting a bit of wood could take a chip out of a propeller.

"I'm good at diving," Jon continued. "I could do it."

"And I could help," said Jan. "I can dive, too." She shook her shell bracelet. "That's how we got these."

"How can we do it without waking them up?" asked Sally. "How can we put the chain on without making a noise?"

"Towels," said Jon, smiling. Sally could see his white teeth gleaming in the darkness. "Two big towels, like. You put them around the propellers first."

"Gee," said Andy, "that's a great idea, can I help, can I?"

"Yes," said Sally sternly. "You can help by being quiet while we make our plans."

They used a length of *Freebooter*'s spare anchor chain—good, strong galvanized steel. It was too long, but they didn't have time to cut it. They used a shackle to make a loop at one end of the chain. The loop was big enough to slip over a propeller.

Sally and the twins swam over to *Black Thunder* with the chain hanging from one of *Freebooter*'s horseshoe life buoys. It was a tense swim, and Sally relaxed only when they arrived at *Black Thunder*'s stern. Nobody taking a casual look out of *Black Thunder*'s wheelhouse would see them there.

Sally found she could almost reach a propeller without putting her head underwater, so the diving wasn't difficult. But Jon's plan to put towels around the propellers first didn't work.

"Darned things keep floating off," he whispered after several attempts. He made a fist and gritted his teeth with frustration.

"Leave the towels, then. Let's just be extra careful to be quiet when we slip the chain over the propeller."

Sally knew how loud things sounded inside a boat when anything outside touched the hull or propellers. Even tiny pistol shrimps on the hull made sharp cracking noises inside. But it was a chance they had to take.

Sally thought she'd better place the chain herself. It wouldn't do to trust anyone else. But Jon just took the chain from her hands and sank below the surface. She was too surprised—and too late—to say anything.

He appeared again after only a few seconds, grinning. "Perfect," he whispered. "No problem."

With one end hooked over the left propeller, Sally and Jan together wrapped the loose end around the right propeller. They popped up, water streaming off their heads, and handed the end to Jon.

He took a breath, disappeared again, and wrapped another turn around the first propeller. The remaining chain dangled straight down.

Sally wanted to wrap it all backward and forward between the two props, just to be sure, but there wasn't time. It must have been nearly 5:00 A.M., she knew, because the sky was beginning to get light. Besides, they were all getting tired. So Jon made one last dive and shackled the chain to itself.

When it was all done, they paddled away from the shelter of the stern very cautiously. Sally had no idea how much noise they'd made, or whether anyone had woken up.

They could soon see, though, that no one was on deck. So they clung to the life buoy and softly swam the fifty yards back to *Freebooter*.

Peter was waiting in the cockpit. He looked agitated. "We were getting worried," he said. "What took so long?"

"Long?" said Sally. "Ten minutes isn't long."

"Nearly half an hour!" said Peter. "I was going to come to look for you."

They clambered aboard and Andy shoved his head up the companionway. "Engine's ready," he announced.

"Can't start it yet," said Sally. "It'll wake them up. We must get past them quietly and out of range. We'll have to sail out. We'll sail behind them."

"Out of range?" Peter repeated. He searched her face for a clue.

"Bullet range. Just in case."

She looked toward the reef, now just visible in the gray light before dawn. She could see the way out to sea. This time the opening through the reef was comfortably wide. But they had to pass *Black Thunder* to reach it.

A tingle of excitement touched her spine. Or was it fear? She shivered. No time to worry. Time to go.

She stood at the tiller and called Peter. "Cut the anchor rope," she told him. "Then raise the jib sail. Do it slowly. But as fast as you can." She hoped that made sense. "And don't make any noise," she added.

"Cut the anchor rope?" Peter could hardly believe his ears. No good sailor cut expensive rope and left behind an anchor that cost five hundred dollars.

"Just do it!" she hissed fiercely. "Now!" It was the only way to escape quickly and silently. It had to be done.

"What was that all about?" whispered Andy as Peter came past the mast.

"She told me to cut the anchor rope."

"Wow! I'm glad I don't have to explain that to Dad."

Sally took a careful look around. Everything was still quiet on *Black Thunder*. The only things moving were Percy and his friend Sam, searching for fish for breakfast.

Peter turned the winch handle on the mast, and

the jib climbed steadily up the forestay. Andy held the bottom of the sail over to one side, so the wind would blow *Freebooter* around to face the open sea.

Freed from her anchor, the yacht started to move slowly through the water.

Then, when the sail was nearly fully up, Peter paused and turned the winch handle backward to get a better grip.

It was a mistake he'd never forget as long as he lived.

In reverse, the winch handle idled back over a noisy ratchet. It was the ordinary kind of boat noise you wouldn't even notice at sea or in harbor.

But here on this deserted island it was alarming. It ripped through the crisp dawn silence as if someone had run along an iron fence with a stick. A dozen loud clacks rang out before he could get himself stopped.

"It's okay," Sally whispered in the startled silence that followed. "Not your fault. I should have remembered."

But her mouth was dry with fright. It couldn't have happened at a worse time.

They were within easy shooting range of *Black Thunder* now. And they were sailing toward her, getting closer all the time.

14

~~~~~~

FREEBOOTER UNDER FIRE

Freebooter's tall jib sail bulged tightly with the cool morning wind and urged the yacht forward. Sally gripped the long tiller so tightly her fingers sank into the ridges in the grain of the wood.

She waved Peter and Andy back to the cockpit, where Jon and Jan were sitting. "Get down low and keep still," she called softly. She swung the tiller so *Freebooter* would miss *Black Thunder*'s stern.

Jon and Jan pulled with all their weight on the jib sheet to keep the sail swelling with power.

Now there were just ten yards to go to pass behind *Black Thunder*. Sally began to think the noise of the winch hadn't woken anybody after all. Still no sign of life there.

Five yards to go. Still nothing. Sally's knuckles were white on the tiller.

They slid silently past the motorboat's stern, holding their breath.

Five yards past—and a man in white shorts and a T-shirt suddenly appeared in the wheelhouse. In his hand he carried a gun.

At that very moment Percy dived into the shallow water in front of *Black Thunder*. He fell with a great splash in his usual untidy fashion, all legs and wings and beak and commotion. One-legged Sam fluttered and hovered overhead, squawking anxiously.

Sally stared at the man in the wheelhouse, just a few yards away. She could almost touch him if she stretched her arm out. Her heart was thumping in her chest, racing out of control.

He was facing away from them, opening the door to the deck on the side *Freebooter* had just come from. He was rubbing his eyes and gazing at Percy and Sam. He hurried to the front of the motor cruiser without taking his eyes off the birds, leaned over the bow, and inspected Percy more closely. He was clearly puzzled that a pelican and a scruffy little sea gull could make a noise like a stick being whacked along an iron fence.

"Just a few more minutes," Sally whispered fiercely. "Don't look this way! Don't look this way!"

"Are we out of range yet?" Andy asked.

"Don't think so."

Sally had no idea how far a handgun could fire. She just knew it was a long way.

After a few more moments the man shook his head slowly and walked briskly back to the wheelhouse. He glanced over to where *Freebooter* should have been—and stopped dead in his tracks, with one foot inside the wheelhouse and one out.

He whirled around and spotted them.

"Hey!" he yelled. "Hey! Come back here!"

They were about seventy-five yards away now and moving steadily toward the sea. He jumped into the wheelhouse, shouted something, and came out again. He started firing his gun. Within seconds the woman was on deck, too. She also had a gun.

"Everybody get down below!" cried Sally. "Start the engine!"

She crouched low in the cockpit, holding the tiller from underneath. More shots rang out behind them.

Then *Freebooter*'s diesel engine began to throb. Sally put it in gear and pushed the throttle lever right over. The yacht lifted her bow and kicked up a boiling, twisting wake. She charged out to sea at seven knots.

Andy rushed up, looking worried. "Is the water coming out?" he asked. "The exhaust water?"

"Get back down!" she shouted. "They're still shooting."

"But—"

"Down with you!"

The shooting stopped while they were going through the gap in the reef. Sally lifted her head cautiously and saw Benito on the foredeck. Gloria was in the wheelhouse, at the controls.

Sally called the others up. "I think they were just firing in the air to frighten us," she said.

"Warning shots, like," said Jon.

"Yes."

"Now they're coming after us," said Jan. "At least, they think they are. Look, look, they've started the engines."

Two puffs of blue exhaust smoke drifted away from *Black Thunder*'s transom. A fraction of a second later they heard the far-off roar of powerful diesel motors. Benito pulled up the anchor. Then he ran back along *Black Thunder*'s side deck to the wheelhouse.

Sally held her breath. They'd be putting her in gear now. The engines would try to turn the propellers.

As *Freebooter*'s crew watched with mounting tension, a spine-tingling noise cut through the air, a split-second, screaming whine of tortured metal. That was followed quickly by the panicky noise of engines revving out of control. Benito ran and looked over the stern. Sally saw him turn toward the wheelhouse and wave his arms hopelessly.

Black Thunder was drifting sideways toward the dangerous reef. The smoke stopped coming out of the exhaust. They had switched the engines off. Engines were no good without propellers.

"Look!" cried Sally. Benito was running forward, lowering the anchor again. "We've done it! We've escaped!"

She relaxed her grip on the tiller for the first time.

Jan let out a great yell and gave Sally such an excited hug that both of them nearly fell over. They sat down unexpectedly side by side with a big thump on the cockpit bench. "We really did it!" cried Jan.

Sally beamed from ear to ear.

"Three cheers!" said Andy, doing a war dance in the cockpit. "Three cheers for Percy and Sam. They made Benito look the wrong way long enough so we could get away." He sighted along the handle of a deck mop and fired imaginary bullets back at *Black Thunder*.

"Can they go anywhere in their rubber dinghy?" asked Peter.

"Not if they've any sense," said Jon. "It's not fit for sea work, like."

"Then they really are trapped on Scorpion."

"Just as we wanted," said Sally.

Now that the sun had risen, she could see the large, high island of Tortuga far away on her right. Crab Island and the other smaller ones still hid behind the morning mist, but she knew they were over to the left, straight across the trade wind, just the same as before. She swung *Freebooter* in that direction, feeling the wind on her face.

Andy jumped to the stern and looked over to make sure the cooling water was spurting out of the exhaust. "Engine's okay," he reported happily. "May be running a bit fast, though."

He was right. Dad didn't like to run the engine at full speed for too long. Sally eased the lever back to the three-quarter mark.

Peter pushed his head up through the hatchway. "Aren't we going to sail?" he asked. "We'd go just as fast with the mainsail up."

He was right, too. That's what Dad would have done. He would have turned the engine off and sailed.

Suddenly, for the first time, Sally's stomach fluttered nervously. They had never sailed *Freebooter* anywhere without Dad. There hadn't been time to worry about it while they were escaping. But now— well, here they were in the open sea, sailing a forty-five-foot yacht on their own. And she was in charge.

Then the spasm of nervousness passed. The sun

felt warm on her shoulders. The sea was calm after a good night's rest and the wind was just right, just enough for a good sail. And the three of them knew how to handle *Freebooter* in any weather. They knew how to put up the sails and reef them. They had sailed thousands of miles in *Freebooter* already.

But still . . . it wasn't quite the same. Things felt very different when you were in charge, and you didn't have anybody to tell you what to do, and you had to trust others to do things right.

And yet . . . Peter was right. She slowed the engine down some more. "C'mon everybody," she yelled. "We're going to raise the mainsail."

She gave the tiller to Jon. The rest of them went to the foot of the mast to haul on the halyard that raised the big white sail, and lifted the heavy boom. When it was nearly up, they wound the halyard around the winch and Peter turned the handle again, around and around, and then backward, to get a better grip. The ratchet rattled away again and they all laughed.

"Hey, listen—it sounds just like a pelican fishing," said Jan.

Andy and Peter giggled.

"C'mon Percy," cried Andy. "Do it for us again."

But Percy ignored them. He was flapping along slowly thirty yards away, looking very bored.

Sally switched off the engine and *Freebooter*

surged quietly over the gentle swells toward Crab Island.

"This is fun," said Jon. "I didn't know it was so easy to steer a big boat like this. Like, it's so simple. Almost like sailing *Gemini*." He paused. His eyes met Jan's.

"I want to see the inside," said Jan suddenly. "I haven't had a look in daylight."

Sally showed her how everything worked. *Freebooter* was mostly built of wood inside her sturdy fiberglass hull. Her pretty, white-painted bulkheads, or cross-walls, had varnished edges. The main cabin was light and airy. The sun shone in through round portholes rimmed with glowing bronze. A beautiful teak table filled the space between the mast and the settee on one side. The table had low flaps on the edges, so plates and cups wouldn't slide off when the yacht heeled over. There were bookshelves and a kitchen and a ship's clock and neat little bunks tucked away under the deck.

"It's fantastic," said Jan. "It's so snug. It's just like a home."

Sally laughed. "It *is* a home. It's our home while we sail around the world."

"You're so lucky."

"It's a bit small sometimes, with four of us on

board," said Sally. "That's why we like to go camping whenever we can."

When they came on deck again, Crab Island was visible on the horizon. The last of the morning mist was swirling high around Lookout Point.

Andy and Peter were keeping watch for other boats while Jon steered.

Sally sat down contentedly in the cockpit. "I'd better get some breakfast going," she said. "You must all be starving."

She yawned and stretched out on the bench. The sunshine poured over her arms and legs in a warm stream. She closed her eyes and turned her face to the sun, seeing the bright blood red of her eyelids. She felt so tired. *Freebooter* was rising and falling soothingly on the swells.

Dimly, she heard Andy yelp, "Hey, hey, we forgot *Gemini*. Where's *Gemini*?"

Jon said something and Andy replied, "Oh, no!"

Then it was Peter's voice, asking about the fender, and Jan's voice explaining how Sally had forgotten to tell them she'd brought it back in *Redwing*, and pretty soon nobody was saying anything and it was all nice and quiet and peaceful. . . .

When she awoke, Andy was talking. His voice was high and very insistent. "But this *is* a special occasion, it *is*. We ran the blockade. We escaped the enemy fire. Our captain is lying wounded in the cockpit. . . ."

Sally propped herself up on one elbow. "What's going on?"

"I'm having chocolate cookies for breakfast," he said.

"Dad said they're only for special occasions," said Peter. "We don't have many. They're supposed to be a special treat."

Sally sat up. She put her arms around her brothers. "Well, I think you're both special," she said. "I think we all deserve a special treat, Jon and Jan, too."

"Good," said Andy, wriggling away and disappearing down the hatch. "I'll bring some more. Anyone for a ginger beer?"

She had slept for about two hours and they were now about halfway to Crab Island, within radio range of the Hurricane Harbor police. Sally switched on the transmitter at the navigation desk.

She pressed the button: "Hurricane Harbor police, this is the sailing yacht *Freebooter*." She paused. What was it that Dad always said? Oh, yes . . . "Do you read, please? Over."

A crisp voice replied almost immediately. "Go to channel twelve, please, *Freebooter*."

She turned the switch to 12 and waited.

"*Freebooter*—this is the port police. Send your message."

"We were kidnapped," said Sally. "They shot at us but we had their fender, now they're stuck on Scorpion, we put a chain around their props and—"

"Hold it, *Freebooter*! Let's take this one thing at a time. Start from the beginning again, please."

It took several minutes to tell the story, even very briefly.

"Watch out for us, *Freebooter*," said the police. "We're coming to meet you."

Sally went on deck to make sure the fender was still in the cockpit. Jon had one foot propped against it.

She picked it up. "As soon as we've handed this over to the police we can go home," she said.

Jon asked, "Why would the police be wanting it?"

"I think there's something inside," said Sally.

"You mean, drugs, like?"

"Maybe. Gloria wanted it very badly. It must be worth quite a lot." She looked at it closely, as she had before, but still could see no way to open it. "I'll be glad to get rid of it," she added. "It's caused enough trouble already. I'll be glad to get back to Crab Island."

She hadn't thought about Crab Island for ages. She hadn't thought about DJ or Daniel, either. She hoped nothing had happened to poor little DJ while they'd been away.

He must be hungry again by now. He must be thinking they'd all deserted him, even Percy. She hoped he hadn't tried to do anything silly like wiggle through the net.

15

~~~~~~

THE SECRET OF THE FENDER

The police arrived an hour later in a fast cutter called *Snapper*. Her hull was painted a smart navy blue and her cabin was white. Two men stepped aboard *Freebooter* to get the full story.

"I'm Inspector Granger," said the taller of the two. "And this is Sergeant Brown."

Sally showed them the fender. Sergeant Brown shook it and felt its weight. He searched in his pocket for a knife and made a slit in the plastic on top of the fender.

The inspector poked a finger in. It came out covered with white powder.

"Coke?" asked the sergeant.

Inspector Granger sniffed the powder and nodded. "More than likely." He looked at *Freebooter*'s crew. "We've been waiting a long time for a break like this."

"Is it the drug?" Andy stood on tiptoe to try to get a better look. "Is it cocaine? Is it?"

"I think so. They'll have to look at it in the laboratory, of course. But I'm pretty sure that's what it is."

He listened carefully to Sally's story of how *White Lightning* ran onto the reef and how the fender floated ashore.

"We know cocaine comes to the islands from Colombia," said the inspector. "We even suspected *Black Thunder*. But we could never find any drugs aboard her."

"Very clever," said Sergeant Brown, nodding his head. "Every time we pulled alongside her, they'd just put the fenders overboard. Who would suspect a fender? What could be more natural on a boat?"

The inspector shook Sally's hand formally. "You've done very well, miss," he said. He ran a quick eye over her crew. "Do you, um, need any help to dock the boat?"

"No thank you," Sally said confidently. "We can manage."

"Do you know the way?"

"Yes."

"I could leave one of my men with you." He looked at her searchingly.

"Thanks, but we're okay."

"Very well, then. We'll see what we can find at Scorpion. We'll be in touch later."

They took the fender aboard *Snapper*. The rumble of her twin diesels changed to a roar. She heeled over as her bow spun around and pointed to Scorpion Island. Then she lifted onto a plane, flinging white spray far out to each side.

Sally waited until they were well on their way. Then she said, "C'mon crew, let's pull the sails in! We're going home."

The last two hours dragged terribly. Nobody said much. They all felt weary and sleepy. Sally steered while they slumped around in the cockpit, yawning and dozing. She looked at them and could see why the inspector had asked if she needed help. Her crew certainly didn't look very trustworthy.

And yet, she thought, looks weren't everything. She hadn't wanted to trust the Geminis when they had offered to take her to Scorpion. But she couldn't have managed in *Redwing* on her own; so she had been *forced* to trust them. And it was thanks to them that she had got the boat and her brothers back.

She hadn't wanted to trust Jon to put the chain around the propeller, either. But he'd done it, anyway. And he'd done it perfectly.

She remembered the time she'd nearly wrecked

Redwing on the reef. Andy had told her to go straight and she hadn't trusted him. But he'd been right.

She'd upset Peter by not trusting him to pull the jib in right. And that was silly, because Peter was a good sailor. It had been his idea to build up the fire to lead them in at night, too.

She thought for a long time about these and other times when she and her brothers had been mad at each other because she wouldn't trust them. And the more she thought about it, the better she realized how Mom had been able to control them and still keep their love.

The answer was quite simple, really. If you wanted people to like you and respect you, you first had to trust them. That's what Mom always had done. And that's what Dad was doing now. He was trusting her to look after her brothers while he was away.

She felt good when she'd worked that out. It was a relief. Now she knew what she had to do. It wasn't going to be easy at first, but at least she knew what she had to do. . . .

When they were close enough to Crab Island to see Fort Redwing they dropped the sails and started the motor.

At the mooring buoy in front of the hotel, Sally

carefully faced *Freebooter* straight into the wind, which she knew was correct.

But she was too cautious. The boat was going too slowly. As they approached the buoy, the wind blew the front of the boat around.

She made another wide circle and came in faster. This time she let Andy look after the gear lever and the throttle while she concentrated on the steering.

He threw the motor into astern at the right moment and revved it up to stop her quickly. Up in the bow, Peter hooked the mooring line with the long pole and brought it aboard.

Jon and Jan helped him pull it in and make it fast around the big wooden Samson post. *Freebooter* was safely moored.

"That's great!" said Sally. She felt very relieved. "Everybody did very well!"

"Well enough for a ginger beer?" asked Andy.

"Sure, if there are enough left," said Sally.

"Six. There are six, I've checked. One for each of you and two for me."

"Andy!"

"Just joking."

"You can have mine if you want," said Peter.

"What's the catch?"

"Washing up."

"One night or two?"

"Two, of course."

"One," said Andy.

"Okay, it's a deal."

While they were bargaining in the cockpit, Sally slipped down into the cabin. She sat at the head of her quarter-berth, her own private bunk inside the little tunnel that ran underneath the cockpit floor. She put her hand down into the tunnel to where she could feel Mom's picture on the crossbeam.

She couldn't see the picture without lying down; but she didn't want to lie down because the others would ask her why she was doing it. This was just as good. She ran her fingers across Mom's picture and her lips moved very slightly as she whispered: "I know how to look after them now, Mom. I promise I won't let you down."

Andy blew the brass foghorn three times to signal that they wanted to come ashore, and after a while a man from the hotel rowed out in a small boat.

They all squeezed in for the short trip to the jetty, where the hotel manager, Mr. Whitely, was dancing with anxiety and dry-washing his hands.

"Did your father say you could take the yacht out?" he asked. "We've been very worried. He didn't tell me. Is it okay?"

Sally got out of the rowing boat and went to

greet him. "Oh, it's fine," she said. "Dad trusts us."

Mr. Whitely smiled thinly. He seemed relieved but not entirely satisfied. As the five of them walked away along the path to Fort Redwing, he said uncertainly: "I do hope it's all right."

"It's okay," Sally shouted back. "It's fine, really." She turned her back deliberately and walked after the others. This was no time for small talk. There were things to be done.

She wanted to see DJ, for a start. It was funny how much she had missed him, even in the middle of all the excitement. He'd need some milk straightaway. Oh—and they'd have to raise the tent again. It seemed so long ago that it had come tumbling down about her ears.

And there was that unfinished business with Andy. But first she was going to sleep. And sleep and sleep.

DJ was indeed hungry. He nearly leaped out of the water with joy when they appeared. He darted around in the shallows like a puppy chasing a ball while they filled his bottles.

Sally let Jon and Jan take turns feeding him. The twins sat down in the shallow water and DJ slid up into their laps while they held his bottle.

"He wiggles," said Jan, laughing delightedly. "He sort of shivers while he feeds."

"He calms down after a bit," said Peter, wading

into the water to give DJ a pat. He knew more about DJ's feeding habits than anybody. "He only wiggles and shoves when he's extra hungry."

Percy floated a little way out in the lagoon, watching them with an expression of disgust.

"Oh, c'mon you old sourpuss!" said Peter, splashing water at him. "Shame on you! You're jealous." Percy glared at him.

They left DJ to finish the rest of the bottles on his own and walked slowly up to the camp. It was time to say good-bye to the twins.

"We'll take you back to your camp in *Redwing* if you like," said Sally.

"No, we'll walk," said Jon. "It's not far, like."

"Twelve minutes exactly," said Jan, looking at the watch around her neck. "We timed it last night when we raided you." She grinned wickedly.

"Why don't you bring your tent over here?" asked Peter. "We can make room."

"Yes, now that we're friends," said Sally.

"And we've still got a boat," said Andy. As soon as he'd said it he was sorry.

Jan's smile disappeared and she turned to Jon. "That reminds me. We need to phone home from the hotel," she said. "We should have done it when we came off *Freebooter*. We must tell Mom and Dad about *Gemini*."

"Maybe they'll want us to come home straightaway, like," said Jon. "They won't be very pleased." He shrugged and looked down at the sand.

They walked off in silence through the bush behind the camp, with their heads bent low.

"I'm sad that they lost their boat," said Andy. "I hope they don't get into trouble. I didn't mean . . ."

Sally felt the sting of salt tears in her eyes as she watched the twins walk away. "I'm sure it'll be all right," she said gruffly. People who grew up on islands, people who grew up with boats, understood about shipwreck. At least, she hoped they did.

In any case, now wasn't the best time to think about these things. They were all exhausted. "It's bedtime," she announced.

"I'm not tired!" Peter and Andy said it in chorus.

"And it's broad daylight," Peter added.

"No arguments," said Sally. "You didn't get any sleep last night. Now go to bed."

"You sound just like Mom used to," said Peter. He pulled a pained face, but he said it affectionately.

Sally smiled happily. She wasn't really like Mom yet. But she was learning. And she was about to show them what she had learned.

16

~~~~~~

FAMILY REUNIONS

Peter was the last one to wake up from his sleep. It was late afternoon and the trade wind had dropped to a gentle breeze. He stood beside Sally outside the tent, rubbing his eyes. Andy was down on the beach, rigging *Redwing* for a sail.

"I'll go and help him," said Peter.

"No, don't!" Sally was surprised at how harsh she sounded. "I've sent him off for his solo."

"The real one? Under sail?"

"Yes." She picked up another potato and started peeling it.

"Aren't you going to watch to see that he does it right?"

"He will. I'm sure he will."

"But . . . you usually . . . he might forget something. . . ." His voice trailed off lamely.

"He'll be just fine," said Sally. "I trust him."

"Aren't you even going to watch?"

"I told you: I trust him. I'm not going to spy on him."

That was the most difficult part—not watching. Not looking up from the potato peeling, not even when she heard Peter whispering fiercely under his breath: "Life jacket! Life jacket!"

Moments later she heard Peter sigh with relief. She looked at the half-finished potato in her hand and started peeling again.

Once, just once—and only after she'd finished the potatoes—she asked: "How's he doing?"

"Great," said Peter. "He's outside the lagoon already."

"That's nice." She dropped the potatoes into the pot in the fireplace and searched in the tent for some cans of stewed meat.

After half an hour *Redwing* appeared off the reef again. Andy was in a high state of excitement.

"Sally! They're circling!" he shouted. "The dolphins are hunting in the Narrows. I saw them, as close as anything, leaping and diving, around and around."

Sally came running down to meet him. "Did you see Daniel?"

"Couldn't tell. There were too many."

"Tell you what," said Sally, "this could be our

big chance. Gosh, but I've been such a dummy! We should have done this in the first place."

"What?"

"The recording of DJ's voice. We should have towed it behind *Redwing* out in the deep water instead of just lowering it over the reef. C'mon. We're going back."

The dolphins had finished their feeding frenzy when *Redwing* arrived for the second time. They were no longer chasing and hunting. Now, with their bellies full of fresh fish, they were playful.

Four came up alongside the dinghy from behind, arched through the bow wave for a moment, and swiftly disappeared ahead. Sally switched on the recording of DJ at full volume and sailed through the widely scattered pod, watching for the black shapes speeding past underwater.

She headed for home and three dolphins followed. Twice she tipped the boat over dangerously as she tried to look back at them, and twice Andy had to balance the boat while she corrected her course.

"Andy, *you* look," she said eventually. "See if you can recognize Daniel. I have to concentrate on steering."

"There's only one now," said Andy calmly. "He's coming up terrifically fast and . . ."

As he said it, a dolphin leaped out of the water at *Redwing*'s stern and landed with a mighty splash halfway to the bow.

"It's her!" cried Sally. "It's her! Did you see the marks on her back?"

"Yes," said Andy matter-of-factly. "But I think you're heading too far—Jibe ho!" he shouted.

Sally ducked and the boom whistled over her head, fetching up with a mighty crash against the shroud.

"Sorry," she said. "Very sorry. But it's Daniel! Daniel's back!"

"Would you like me to steer?"

"Well, yes, all right. Straight back to the camp, okay?"

Sally pulled the recorder a little closer to the boat and Daniel came back in a big circle, swimming excitedly.

"Oh, hurry, Andy, do hurry!"

"I'm doing my best," said Andy huffily, "but it isn't easy with you bouncing around like that."

After a few minutes they came to the passage through the reef. Andy hardened in the mainsail and then reached over to pull in the jib. Sally was too busy with Daniel to attend to the crew's job.

As *Redwing* turned closer to the wind for the final tricky stretch through the gap, neither of them remembered the net.

The lowered centerboard hit the net square on. It stretched and then floated free of the coral. *Redwing* checked her way momentarily and then surged forward again.

Sally turned around quickly. "What was that?"

Andy looked over the side and saw the floats clunking alongside. "The net. I forgot about the net." *Redwing* sailed slowly toward the beach, dragging the net with her.

"No matter," said Sally. "I think it's going to be okay."

She was right.

Daniel flashed past *Redwing* into the lagoon. With swift flicks of her tail she headed for the shallows. DJ squeaked delightedly and swam in a tight circle with her.

Peter, who was fishing on the rocks next to DJ's nursery, heard the splashing and thought DJ was being attacked. But as he ran toward them he recognized Daniel.

"She's home!" he shouted. "It's Daniel."

"We know!" Sally and Andy dragged *Redwing* up onto the beach and left her with sails flapping.

As they waded into the lagoon, Daniel and DJ did one last circle. Then, like arrows from a bow, they headed straight for the open ocean.

As they passed through the reef they leaped into the air together in a graceful arc, their bodies close together, and dived neatly into the deep water with hardly a splash.

"They're saying good-bye," said Sally. "They'll be okay now."

The words came out strangely. Her throat was suddenly tight. To her surprise, her eyes filled with tears and she had to blink quickly to clear them.

It had all happened so quickly and unexpectedly. She had trusted Andy. And he had found Daniel.

Andy and Peter did a dance on the spot and waved enthusiastically.

"Good thing I deliberately hit the net so Daniel could come in," said Andy.

"Deliberately?"

"Well, sort of."

"Ha! I bet."

"Let's celebrate," said Sally.

"How?"

"The usual way. Ginger beer."

They sat close together on the beach, passing the bottle back and forth.

"I have a toast," said Peter. "To Daniel and DJ."

"To Daniel and DJ." Sally and Andy repeated it after him.

"Long life and good fishing," added Andy.

"And here's another toast," said Peter. "To the Dolphins."

"We just did that," said Andy.

"No, it's us. The Dolphins. It's our new name. How do you like it?"

"I like that much better than the Freebooters," said Sally.

"Hurray for the Dolphins!" said Andy. "I'm a Dolphin! I'm a Dolphin!"

"Well, you can swim," said Peter. "That's a good start."

"I can do Turk's heads, too. I told you they're magic."

For a long time they sat quietly and looked out to sea, beyond the surging reef, but no more dolphins jumped for them that day. Or needed to.

Inspector Granger arrived late in the afternoon, looking hot and flushed. He had walked around from the hotel.

"Good news," he said, taking off his cap and sitting on the grass in front of the tent. "We caught your drug runners. They're in jail awaiting trial. They didn't even see us coming. They were too busy trying to saw through the chain around their propellers." He laughed and looked at Sally. "That was a clever piece of work."

"What happens to *Black Thunder* now?" asked Peter.

"She's ours. We towed her back. Any boat found

to be carrying illegal drugs is taken by the police. It's the law. She'll make a fine new patrol boat—thanks to you."

"She'll need new propellers," said Sally.

"And fenders," said Inspector Granger. "We slit open every one on board. Two others were filled with cocaine. But new fenders and propellers is a cheap price to pay."

"How much are the drugs worth?" asked Sally.

"About a hundred thousand dollars, we estimate—and this is the point of my visit: There's a five-thousand-dollar reward. I have a check."

"For us?"Andy whooped with joy.

The inspector looked a little embarrassed. "Yes, it's for you. Unfortunately, however, the law says it must be paid to an adult." He hesitated. "It's not how I would do things, you understand. But I have to follow the law."

"What adult?" said Sally.

"I thought your father would be the right one. The check is made out to him. When does he return?"

"Tomorrow."

"In that case, perhaps I could leave the check with you to give to him. The law doesn't say I can't do that. You can surprise him."

"He won't believe his eyes," said Sally.

"I think he will, miss," said Inspector Granger, putting on his cap and standing up stiffly. "It's his ears he won't believe, when he hears the story."

They were ready and waiting on the hotel jetty for the four o'clock ferry the next day. They had packed up the camp and transported everything back aboard *Freebooter*.

The twins' parents had come to fetch them and take them back to Hurricane Haven, so Fort Redwing was deserted.

Sally made sure they left no plastic or glass. She let Peter bury paper and cardboard, but everything else was brought back and put in the hotel's big garbage bins. Andy raked over the sand with a palm branch and they left the campsite just as they had found it.

Dad was on the hotel ferry. Sally could see him waving long before it arrived. He had gifts for them, which he unpacked when they were aboard *Freebooter*.

Peter got a pair of brass-and-stainless-steel chart dividers that you could open and close with one hand. Andy got a blue baseball cap with gold braid on it and the words CHIEF ENGINEER. Sally got a pewter bookmark in the shape of an anchor.

Then Sally gave him his present. He stared at

the check. "What on earth . . . ?" And they all began to talk at once.

Eventually, after much going back to start at the right place, Dad understood the whole story, about the twins and the cat, about Daniel and DJ, and about the smugglers and *Black Thunder.*

"My word, but you have been busy while I've been away," he said. "And brave, too. Well done, all of you. I'm very, very proud of you. A captain couldn't have a better crew. Or a richer one, come to think of it. How do you plan to spend the check?"

"We talked about that," said Sally. "We want to buy a new catamaran for Jon and Jan so they can sail to their camp again."

"Good idea. You owe it to them. Without their help you couldn't have rescued your brothers. But what about the rest?"

"Well, we think it will just about pay for a new anchor, some chain, some rope, a pair of rubber gloves, and some milk powder," said Sally. "And if there's any left over I think we should open a savings account and keep it for emergencies."

"Like hospital bills for dolphins?"

"Yes." She giggled.

"I agree." Dad looked at her proudly. "Your mother was a very canny woman," he said. "She was clever with money. You're turning out to be your mother's daughter."

Dad changed into his shorts and a T-shirt. He sat in the cockpit and let the afternoon trade wind ruffle his hair and blow between his bare toes.

Sally came to sit beside him. "There's still two weeks before the beginning of hurricane season," he said. "We don't have to leave the West Indies until then. Would you like to invite Jon and Jan for a cruise of the islands on *Freebooter* while they wait for their new boat?"

Sally hugged him. "They'd love it!"

"Well you'd better phone them from the hotel. Give them the good news." He looked at her carefully. "You know," he said, "you seem to have grown while I've been away. It's a funny thing. You don't look any bigger, but you seem to have grown. Isn't that strange?"

Sally felt warm and happy. She was going to say that she had grown inside, where he couldn't see it. She was going to say she had learned something very difficult—to trust others.

But Dad hadn't finished. "And talking about strange," he continued, "can you explain why we have a grumpy pelican sitting on the foredeck, a one-legged sea gull on top of the mast, and six Turk's heads on the tiller?"